MIRROR IMAGE SEDUCTION

FELINE SHIFTERS DOWN UNDER
BOOK 1

KHLOE WREN
TAMSIN BAKER

To our real-life mates, Steve and David, thank you for putting up with all our craziness!
xo
Khloe & Tamsin

CHAPTER ONE

Heat flushed Dylan's cheeks as his temper rose. No bloody way were they going to be sidelined for something this important. He cracked his knuckles, relishing the sound of the joints popping.

"Why the hell can't we go help?"

The burly man standing before him with his arms crossed, looking all smug, was seriously close to having his front teeth knocked out.

"So sorry, boys, only professionals on this one. And last time I checked, wiping the butts of baby animals at the zoo doesn't qualify you."

A growl left Dylan's lips as he took a step forward, clenching his fists by his sides. He didn't get far before his brother's warning sounded in his head.

"He's not worth the trouble, brother. Step back."

With a shuddering breath, Dylan forced his hands to unclench. Ryan was right, of course. Punching Luke in the face wouldn't help their cause, even if it would have made him felt a whole lot better. Stupid prick. Bastard thought he was so special with his Park Ranger certification. Pfft, everyone knew cheetahs were faster than lions. Always had been, always would be.

Dylan allowed Ryan to move in front of him to take over talking to Luke.

"C'mon, Luke, this isn't the time for a pissing match. A little boy is lost, and there's one hell of a storm front coming in."

A loud growl rumbled from Luke. "Don't tell me how to do my job, Ryan. I know exactly what's at stake. That's why it's being left to the professionals. We don't have time to go looking for any civilians that get themselves lost while searching for Cameron. Now if you two would go back to where you came from, I could go do something useful."

Red-hot rage clouded Dylan's vision. He really wanted to claw out Luke's throat now. Pompous dickhead was so full of himself now he was a professional. The only thing he was an expert at was being a pain in the ass.

Dylan watched over Ryan's shoulder as Luke turned his back on them and stomped away like he was king of the world or some shit.

"Please let me hurt him, Ry."

Ryan shook his head, and his shoulders shook as his brother chuckled.

"Why bother? You two have been going at each other for ten years, and all it ever does is piss off our parents and his."

Dylan sighed and rubbed a hand over the dark stubble on his jaw. His twin had a good point.

"Yeah, okay. So, what are we going to do? We're not really going to sit this out, are we?"

Now that Luke had disappeared from view, Ryan turned to face him with a smirk.

"Of course not. While the professionals are busy making their plans, we'll go in and sniff out the lad. What's the bet we'll be back with him before they even finish their damn meeting?"

Every ounce of anger drained from Dylan's body and was replaced with excitement as he grinned at his twin and rubbed his hands together.

"Now that's a plan I can get behind. Let's go."

He turned to jog over to the nearby bush when Ryan's groan had him pausing.

"Think, Dylan. We can't let them see us go into the park. Come back to the car and we'll drive around to another entrance, then head in. Let Luke assume we've gone home like he wants us to. Stupid lions are so caught up with their need to stick to every policy and procedure, he won't even consider that we'd just run off into the bush."

Adrenaline tingled along Dylan's nerves as he forced himself to slowly stroll back to their car. They were so going to show those idiot lions how this shit was done.

The moment the doors were shut on the car, Ryan cranked the engine and they rolled out onto the dirt track leading out of the park.

"What information do you have on Cameron?"

Fortunately, Ryan had been standing behind Luke at the gas station when the call came through on Luke's radio, so there was a good possibility his twin had heard the whole report.

"He's a four-year-old city kid. He was with his family on his first camping trip. His parents had trouble getting their tent set up, and by the time they got it sorted, Cameron had disappeared. As they were doing a thorough search around the campsite, they called the police. That was about half an hour ago."

A growl escaped Dylan's throat as his shoulders tensed. "Idiot city slickers. Didn't they check the forecast before they headed out? That storm is a bad one, and it's going to hit before nightfall. I can feel it."

Ryan sighed. "Yeah, I know. Guess they were just looking for a family holiday and got more than they bargained for. I'm sure camping sounded like fun when they left home this morning. He's so young—that half hour would be feeling like a week to both the boy and his parents."

Dylan grimaced as he thought about the little kids he'd seen with their parents at the zoo where he worked. At that age, kids had a lack of awareness and understanding of the world and were too young to be anywhere alone.

"A four-year-old isn't not going to have many survival skills either. We have to find him. Which campground did he wonder off from?"

He hoped it was one that didn't have any steep cliffs or water holes close by.

"Wallaby Ridge. I'll park just up here a bit, and we'll take the fire trail that runs around behind it. We should be able to pick up his scent easily enough."

Yeah, true that.

Silence filled the car for the rest of the short trip, and Dylan's heart thumped steadily in his chest as he readied himself for their search and rescue mission. Once the vehicle stopped, Dylan wasted no time in using his magic to flash to his cheetah form. He arched his back before stretching out, relishing the feel of his body transforming into something so much faster and more agile. Damn, it felt good to be in his feline form. He glanced over at his brother.

"Let's do this."

Ryan pushed himself hard to sprint at top speed, his muscles burning as his legs pumped hard. They needed to find Cameron, and quickly. The young boy would be terrified, and if he was crying, he could easily misstep and go over a cliff. Ryan could sense his brother to his right, moving as fast as he was. The wind pushed his whiskers back, and the bush rushed by in a blur of green and brown. Ryan loved running flat out like this, and despite the dire circumstances, joy filled him as they crossed great distances at high speed. They rarely risked entering the park in their animal form. It was much safer to go spend time in the open plain zoo with the other non-shifter cheetahs when they felt feline urges. It was great because he loved being able to be true to his nature without concern of being caught, but it wasn't the same as the unlimited space here in the park.

When he neared the campground, he slowed to a stop and took a few deep breaths to calm his wildly beating heart.

"Start sniffing, brother."

"Yes, sir!"

Ryan shook his head. Dylan was always such a smartass and a total hothead. He and Dylan were mirror image twins, but opposite in behavioral characteristics. Ryan was right-handed, while Dylan was a lefty. As cheetahs, they had the same markings, just in reverse. And when it came to their personalities, their mother had always said that Ryan was the ice to Dylan's fire. She was right, not that Ryan minded. What they had worked. They were never meant to be individuals, but a team. Two halves of a whole.

"You going to quit standing around, wasting time like a lion and help me find this kid?"

"Shut up. I'm sniffing."

Dammit, what a time to get caught up in his head. He put his snout to the ground and began searching for the boy's distinct scent. While they didn't know Cameron, they would be able to identify the smell of a young male human when they found it. He hoped there hadn't been too many kids around this campground lately. Fortunately, they'd had a series of storms in the past few weeks, so most campers had gone elsewhere in the state for their adventure.

The sweet smell of human teased his nose, and he took a deeper breath. Yep, young male human.

"Hey, Dylan. I've got a trail here."

A moment later his twin was with him, and they sniffed around the area.

"It's slightly stronger to the west. C'mon."

Without a word, they both continued following the scent. Ryan's tail twitched in the breeze as they continued weaving through the bush. It felt so good to be doing something useful with their skills and getting one up on the lions while they were at it was an added bonus. For a good ten minutes they wove around the trees and scrub, following the boy's trail. Ryan guessed from the path he'd taken, that Cameron had followed an animal before realizing he was lost and panicked. A lump rose in his throat the further west they went. He knew a steep cliff was up ahead, and he prayed the child hadn't fallen down it.

Dylan had moved in front of Ryan by several feet, so when Ryan heard him whine a tortured sound, he sprinted to find his brother across the cleared area atop the cliff.

"What happened?"

"I've found him."

Ryan grimaced at his brother's tone as he came to stop beside him at the top of the cliff. He stretched to see over the edge and stiffened when he saw Cameron, his chest tightening with fear. He could hear the boy's sniffles as he cried, and they tore at his heart. At least he's alive. He was clinging to one of the few trees that had grown on the steep incline.

"Guess he slipped and fell down the slope."

"Easy to do if he was crying and not watching where he was walking."

"The rocks look loose in places, but if we follow this solid rock edge down, we'll come up just beneath him. We'll need to be quick. You got any ideas?"

"You're right, we have to do this thing fast. Cameron is already scared. I vote we just snatch him on our way past."

"Think, Dylan. He's gripping that tree. You could tear the kid's arm off or snap his neck if you try to wrench him from the tree. No child is going to trust a wild animal. And it's too dangerous to even attempt it as a human Do you think he would be able to hear us from here?"

"I don't know. Probably not. He's a fair way down, and the wind is starting to pick up. I can smell that storm coming. We need to do something now."

He knew Dylan was right, but he was struggling to formulate a plan. Where was a damn lion when you needed one? They were so organized and had some great rescue skills, although, they'd probably still be planning when the rain started coming down.

"Only thing I can think of is if we push a thought into his mind. Tell him we're here to help and to trust us. He's gotta be so damn scared by this point, he'll think he's dreaming or something. Then we run down there and grab him."

Ryan nodded. Dylan's idea was the best option they had.

"Cameron, can you hear me?"

"Daddy?"

Even with the wind, Ryan's sensitive ears picked up the boy's response.

"No, buddy, I'm not your daddy. My name is Ryan, and along with my brother, Dylan, we're going to come get you and take you to your parents. Okay?"

He saw the child's head nod.

"My brother and I are special, Cameron. We have some magic that allows us to turn into big cats. Can you look up to the top of the hill for me? See us? The two big, spotty cats?"

Ryan waited patiently until the boy looked up at them, then down again quickly.

"We're going to run past you in a minute and I need you to let go of the tree when I tell you to, okay? When you let go, you'll land on my back. I need you to hang onto my fur. Don't worry about hurting me, you won't. I need you to take a good grip as we need to run the rest of the way down. Can you do that for me, buddy?"

"I want my mummy!"

"I know you do, Cameron. But we can't take you to her until we get you down off this cliff. Can you do what I asked?"

"O-okay."

Ryan took a deep breath then burst down the cliff face toward the boy, following the solid fissure of rock over to the tree.

"Now, Cameron! Drop onto my back."

His every muscle was tense as he waited for the light weight of the boy to land on him. When he finally felt two small fists pull tight on his fur around his neck, he sighed in relief and continued down the slope, listening to the loose rocks and debris tumble down behind him. Now, they just needed to get back to the campground and return Cameron to his parents or the official rescue party without being seen. Regardless of what happened, Ryan knew the lions would know who'd helped the boy, and there would be hell to pay when they next saw each other.

Ryan also knew Dylan was going to have the time of his life when that happened, because it'd give him a chance to take a shot at Luke.

CHAPTER TWO

"Are you ready, Cameron? You're such a brave boy for helping me like this." Lacey smiled at the gorgeous little boy before her, his recently brushed blond hair and shining blue eyes a testament to how resilient kids really were.

"Yep."

Lacey took out her voice recorder and placed it on the low coffee table between Cameron, his mother and herself. She pressed record before she sat down in a comfy leather chair.

"So, Cameron, tell me what happened last week when you went camping."

The boy crossed his arms with a humph. "I didn't get to go camping. After I fell down that hill, Mummy and Daddy made me come home."

A chuckle rose in her throat, but Lacey held it in and grinned instead, trying her best to be as professional as possible. This was one of her first real stories at the Melbourne Herald, and she wanted to make a good impression on her superiors.

"If you didn't get to go camping, what were you doing before you fell? Were you having a good day?"

The little cherub looked up at his mother with a pleading look. The woman nodded to her son as she ran her hands through his hair. "Go on, sweetie. You can tell Lacey about the whole day, if you like."

"But I've already told this story. Over and over! And no one ever believes me."

Lacey bit her lip and hoped her begging expression would be deciphered correctly by his mother.

"I know, sweetie. But Lacey's from a newspaper in town, and she really wants to write about what happened to you, and you'll have your picture in the paper and everything. Wouldn't that be fun?"

He heaved a sigh like a man would. It was probably the exact sigh his father made, and this time Lacey did laugh, glancing at his mother to share a smile. He was adorable.

"Well, Mummy and Daddy took me to the gramins."

"The Grampians," his mother corrected, and her son shot her a disgruntled look.

"The Grampins. And I saw a bird that was real pretty, so I followed it."

Lacey sat forward on her chair and nodded. "What color was it?"

"Oh, it was blue and red. Then its friend came, and they flew away."

Oh, dear. That was when he must have gotten distracted.

"So, you followed the birds, and what happened next, Cameron?"

He began to fiddle with his hands and looked down into his lap. Poor little thing probably had nightmares about getting lost.

"I went through some trees and found some cool rocks. Then, I didn't know which way to go, and I got scared."

His bottom lip quivered, and Lacey rushed to get to the important part of the interview.

"You must have been so frightened, Cameron, and so brave. When you slipped over the cliff, what happened then? We're all so interested to know how you got down all by yourself."

"Oh, I didn't get down by myself."

Lacey looked at his mother, and she gave a roll of her eyes.

"Cameron has a wild imagination."

"No, Mummy, it's true. Why won't you believe me? No one believes me."

Cameron huffed as he crossed his little arms again. Lacey bounced on her chair a time or two then stopped, heat rising in her cheeks when she realized how foolish she must look. She was twenty-four but felt like a child herself sometimes.

"Tell me, Cameron. Doesn't matter how silly. I want to know what happened."

Cameron looked between his mother and her, and finally his mum gave a nod and a sigh for him to continue.

Cameron slid off the couch and held out his arms.

"I rode a spotty cat who was this big." He stretched his arms out even further, and Lacey laughed.

"A cat? What sort of cat?"

Cameron darted off across the room and came back with a large book.

"This one." He opened the shiny cover and flicked through a few pages before pointing with a gleeful expression at a large cheetah. Tan in color with beautiful black spots all over its body, the cheetah was an incredible marvel of speed and strength in an animal. She'd always loved big cats, and at school had done a project on cheetahs. She remembered a few things about them.

"Did you know they can't roar like lions? And that they purr like normal cats!"

"Ah, no. I didn't know that." Lacey didn't know what else to say. How was that even possible? There were a number of cheetahs in captivity at the open range zoo near the Grampians, but they were carnivores and would have ripped the boy to shreds if one found him, assuming his story was actually true. And if a cheetah had escaped from the zoo, surely she'd have heard about it through the newspaper. Wouldn't she?

No, it was impossible.

"That's incredible, Cameron. Tell me more about the rescue. How did you get this scratch on your face?" She pointed to a red gash on his cheek that looked to be healing nicely.

"A tree scratched me when I fell off the cliff."

Lacey lifted her eyes to his mother's face, lifting her eyebrows in question.

"Ah, we think at least that part is true. The rescue team followed a trail and found a little blood and a piece of Cameron's shirt attached to a tree partway down a steep cliff face."

Her eyes shimmered with tears, and Lacey's chest tightened. What a horrible thing for a mother to experience. The sheer terror of losing him and then the relief of his return, only to find out that he could have died yet didn't. Lucky didn't cover this kid's experience.

"Then you were amazingly lucky, Cameron. Not many people survive a fall down a cliff and a fight with a cheetah, too!" She smiled and nudged him, and he stared at her as though confused.

"No. They saved me. I was down the cliff hanging onto the tree, and I could hear him talking to me. He said he was going to run down and save me. All I had to do was grab his fur and hang on."

His serious little face and the solemn tone made goosebumps rise on Lacey's arms. She rubbed the flesh with her hands, wishing she'd worn a warmer top.

"And did you?"

He nodded. "Yep. And he ran me back to the camp. No one was there, but they said they had to go, that they couldn't get caught. They made me promise to stay until Mummy and Daddy came back. I was so hungry, I ate everything in my lunch box. Didn't I, Mummy?"

She tousled his hair and smiled gently. "Yes, you did, honey. You were a good boy."

"So, do you believe me, Miss Lacey?"

She smiled down at the adorable boy. "Of course I do, Cameron."

That seemed to please him, and he beamed a huge grin before he turned to his mother. "Can I go and play now?"

Lacey grabbed her camera and motioned for him to move back.

"Just one picture for the paper before you run off, if I can, mate?"

Cameron pouted but moved to stand still as she'd directed him to.

"Okay, but can I have the book, too? To show the cat picture?"

"Yeah, sure." Why not? If she had to write this story, then she needed proof that the child believed it.

Cameron picked up the book and grinned while pointing to the cheetah.

Lacey snapped off a few photos on her new digital camera, and by the time she'd lowered her arms, Cameron had already dropped the book to the couch and run off in the opposite direction, out of the room.

"He won't change his story no matter how hard we try to explain that what he's saying is impossible."

Lacey shrugged, checking over the few photos she'd taken and smiling at the beautiful image the young boy made. His cheeky grin would win any woman's heart.

"Children create stories all the time. He has a great imagination. It's most likely just his mind's way of coping with the traumatic events."

She turned and smiled at Cameron's mother, whose furrowed brow showed more concern than the situation seemed to warrant.

"But how did he really get off that slope and back to camp? I mean, he couldn't find it initially when he got lost. Why would he be able to find it afterwards?"

It was a good question, but Lacey didn't have an answer.

"The most important thing is that you got him back. If some magical creature carried him home for you, then it's probably best for your sanity to simply thank the universe for it and move forward. You'll drive yourself crazy with questions if you're not careful."

Cameron's mother nodded and pulled out her phone. "True. Can I show you something before you go?"

Lacey nodded as she turned off her recorder and began to pack up her things. This was going to be one weird story to write, but she'd have fun with it. Should she dare say a guardian angel had been watching over him?

"I took a photo to show the rangers, but they just ignored it. Tried to tell me it was from one of the search dogs, but I saw the dogs they had out there. None of them were this big. But it's not really possible, is it?"

She handed Lacey her phone, and Lacey's mouth hung open as her eyes absorbed the picture of a big animal footprint in the mud.

"Is that..." It could be a cheetah, she supposed. It was certainly large enough. She'd have to do some research. "Would you mind sending that to me? I'd love to look into this a bit more."

"Yeah, sure." Cameron's mum put the photo into a text message and handed the phone back to Lacey. "Just type your number in."

Lacey did as she asked, her belly fluttering a little as she stared at the paw print once again.

"Please save my number and call me if you or Cameron remember anything else."

The woman smiled properly for the first time since Lacey had arrived as she stood to walk with Lacey to the front door.

"Of course, and thanks for covering Cameron's story. It was really nice of you to come so far to talk to us."

"No, not at all. It was really great to meet you both."

Lacey made one more quick check of her handbag to make sure she had everything and called out her goodbye to Cameron. The little boy came hurtling through the house towards her, skidding to a stop just before he bumped into her. She laughed as she squatted down and got onto the same level with him.

"Hey, mate, where's the fire?"

"No fire! Do you really believe me?"

Lacey put her hand on her chest. "Cross my heart, I believe you."

"I remembered something else, but it's a secret. Do you wanna know the secret?"

Lacey nodded solemnly and leaned forward when he cupped his hands around his mouth so he could bring his lips to her ear.

"They said not to tell, but you believe me, so I'll tell you. Their names were Dylan and Ryan. They were brothers."

He stepped back and gave her a triumphant grin. "But you promise you won't tell anyone I told you, right?"

Lacey shook her head, keeping her smile in place even as a tingle ran down her spine. "Of course not."

"Cool." He waved as he tore off through the house once again.

Feeling a little like she was in a trance, Lacey thanked his mother once more and left the house with a wide grin spread across her face. She bounced down the outside steps and walked over to her car.

What an incredible story this was going to be. Magical cats in the Grampians. She could just see the headline now. She giggled to herself and let out a happy sigh. Her life was finally heading in the right direction, and she had an unusual and uplifting story as her first ever solo journalism piece.

Her phone buzzed, and Lacey lifted it to see who had messaged her this time. Her stomach dropped along with her heart rate as she saw the name of her ex-boyfriend on the screen.

"Damn."

When he'd first started his games, she'd blocked his number, but it was never more than a day or two before he'd have a new number and be back to blowing up her phone. She'd lost count of how many new numbers he'd gone through before she'd given up wasting her time trying to block him.

She pulled open her car door and slid in before she slammed it shut. Maybe it was time to get a restraining order sworn out against him. Her mother had urged her to get one after they first broke up, but Lacey hadn't wanted to give him a reason to escalate his behavior. She'd read some horrific stories about women who were beaten, raped or murdered after they got restraining orders on their exes.

Pissed off that he'd ruined yet another good mood, she turned the key with a heavy sigh before she put the car in gear and pressed her foot against the accelerator.

Time to go home.

CHAPTER THREE

Still getting used to his human form, relief spread through Dylan as he slid onto the stool at the bar with a groan. Whenever he spent a long period of time as a cheetah, it always took him a number of hours to readjust after the shift back.

"Man, do I need a drink."

His twin pulled up next to him as Trent came over to serve them, a glint of humor in his eyes.

"You know watching you two is spooky as hell, right?"

The familiar bartender was shaking his head as he rested his hands on the bar and stared at them.

"Why's that?"

"Not only are your looks a mirror image, you move opposite, too. Like just now? One of you got on your stool from the right, while the other was from the left. Never seen anything like it before I met the two of you."

Dylan cracked a lopsided grin at Trent as Ryan cleared his throat to reply. His brother defended their anomaly every time someone said something. Mostly, Dylan just laughed it off ... or played it up to really annoy whoever was dumb enough to comment on it.

"Approximately twenty-three percent of identical twins are mirror-image twins. It's not that rare. But I will admit, it's fun freaking people out. You should see us when we're actually trying to mess with someone's head."

Trent chuckled a little. "I can only imagine how insane you two drove your parents while growing up."

Dylan barked out a laugh. "We have seven older brothers, mate. I'm pretty sure our folks were insane before we were even thought about!"

The way the bartender's eyes peeled wide had both Dylan and Ryan belly laughing.

"I hope you're joking, but I'm pretty sure you're not. Nine kids? All boys." He paused to shudder. "I don't want to know anything else. Okay, what can I get you both?"

"Just our usual beers tonight. Thanks, mate."

Dylan watched in silence as Trent efficiently went about getting their beers. Dylan left Ryan to pay as he snatched up his glass and took a deep swallow of the cool, amber liquid.

"Oh, yeah. That's what I'm talking about."

After the rescue just over a week ago, they'd arrived home to find their father waiting on the front porch for them. He'd heard about the search and recovery on the radio and had been pissed at them for exposing themselves. Their punishment was having to spend an entire week at the zoo in cheetah form, where they couldn't cause any more trouble.

They were lucky that their parents had settled so close to an open range zoo. All fifty or so animals were in huge pastures in a total of nearly fifteen-hundred hectares. They kept the carnivores like the lions and the cheetahs separated from the herbivores like the giraffes. But as a rule, they did a great job at providing a large, animal-friendly zoo. You needed to go on a forty-minute bus safari just to see everything.

"Uh huh. That sure does hit the spot."

Yep, he completely agreed with his twin. In cheetah form at the zoo, they'd been on a diet of water and raw meat. While it provided all the nutrients they needed, and in animal form they didn't have a problem with uncooked food, it was boring and repetitive. Although, he did have fun chasing the odd rabbit or kangaroo that was dumb enough to hop into the cheetah field at the zoo.

"We need to scrub out that water trough when we get to work Monday."

Ryan laughed at him.

"Yeah, that was not the best tasting, was it?"

Dylan mock shuddered, the memory of the taste of the muddy water enough to make him gag.

"It's going to take at least three days before I can taste anything other than sand."

Ryan rolled his eyes, "Oh, cut the crap. It wasn't that bad, Mr. I'm-a-chef-now-so-all-food-must-be gourmet."

Dylan shrugged.

"You know I like the finer things. And really, why settle for scraps when you can have a juicy steak? There has to be some benefit in being able to shift form. I happen to believe cooking one's food to perfection is one of them."

"I know you do. I'll admit I'm glad to be back on two feet again. An entire week is way too long to be solely in either form."

Silence filled the space between him and his twin. As shifters, they needed to spend time in both their human and feline forms regularly. Being stuck in one form for any length of time was not healthy. They lost themselves to that form and found it difficult to merge once again with the other. Like now, they were struggling a little to keep from following their cheetah instincts. At least he was, so he assumed Ryan was dealing with the same animalistic desires. Dylan suddenly shuddered. His skin was super sensitive without his feline's thick fur, and he felt every little brush of air. Damn air conditioning. His stomach began grumbling for more food than he'd allowed himself to eat for lunch. As a cheetah, he ate a massive meal every three days or so. Readjusting to three small meals every day took at least a few days each time. Their father certainly knew how to choose punishments. Maybe coming out to the pub on their first night as humans wasn't the best idea, especially considering their lack of control over their baser urges.

"Well, look who's come out of hiding at last."

A growl rippled up Dylan's throat, cutting off his immediate response. Yep, definitely shouldn't have come out tonight.

"Piss off, Luke. We're in no mood to put up with your shit tonight."

"What? The great and mighty Dylan and Ryan aren't gloating?"

Dylan clenched his teeth, spun around and slid from his stool to get into Luke's face. Being a lion, Luke was large and a lot broader than Dylan. Cheetahs were sleeker, more athletic than the lion's bodybuilder stature. But Dylan could take him. He knew he could, because he'd done it before. Speed and agility won over brute strength. Most times.

"You know full well we won't say a damn word about it. We went in and did what needed doing, while you were sitting on your ass thinking about it. As usual."

Luke shoved his shoulder, hard, and Dylan growled, not giving him an inch.

"I was following the rules. You know? Those things that are put in place to make everything run smoothly? The things you always ignore."

"We got the job done. That storm was coming in, and if we'd waited for you to finish following all your rules, it would have hit the range and Cameron would have been washed down that cliff along with a torrent of water. I don't believe that would have ended well for the lad, do you?"

Ryan's strong fingers gripped his arm and pulled. He held his ground, but with one hard tug, his brother got him off balance and dragged him back toward their stools.

He shook his brother's hand off as he glared at the agitated lion before him. This wasn't going to end well. Luke was clearly looking for a fight, and Dylan was holding onto his temper by a thin thread.

Finally, Ryan sucked in a deep breath and spoke up.

"Here's an idea, Luke. How about you just say, 'thank you' and we'll all move on? Picking a fight about it isn't going to do anything, and you know it."

Luke snarled at Ryan.

"You're too much of a pussy to fight me anyhow, Ryan. You always leave it to your twin. And a fight would certainly help me de-stress, which I need, especially after my day of dealing with a fucking reporter crawling up my ass."

"What for?" Ryan asked as Dylan tilted his head in question.

Luke glared fire and daggers. "Over the fact Cameron is sticking to his story that two big, spotty cats rescued him. Maybe I should have just given little Miss Reporter your mobile numbers. Let you deal with the mess you've made."

Dylan grimaced a little and looked away from the man before him. He'd hoped the boy would think he'd been dreaming or something. Hell, who took anything a four-year-old said as truth? Ryan had another go at placating Luke.

"Luke, honestly, we wouldn't have done the rescue in feline form if it wasn't absolutely necessary. That slope was too steep, and there were too many loose rocks and debris. We didn't intend to cause any issues for you. We were simply attempting to save a scared little boy before he slipped and fell, probably to his death."

Dylan rolled his eyes and flexed his biceps and shoulders. He didn't know why his twin was trying so hard to talk their way out of this when Dylan was more than willing to solve things with a good old-fashioned throwdown with the guy. His animal instincts were flaring on high alert and needed an outlet. Apparently, Luke was in a similar state of mind.

Luke stormed up to stand in front of Ryan, his nostrils flaring. Dylan growled, and when Luke made the mistake of grabbing a fistful of his brother's shirt, he pounced.

That was a mistake, asshole.

Dylan shoved Luke's shoulder so that the prick faced away from Ryan. He pulled back his arm and quickly landed a punch to the guy's jaw. The sound of his fist cracking against thinly veiled bone had his senses buzzing, so much so, that he barely felt the sting in his knuckles. He heard Ryan's sigh as he attempted to land a second punch. Dylan growled when Luke blocked the blow before delivering one of his own. As Luke's fist slammed against his ribs, Dylan's breath rushed from his lungs. Damn, that hurt. A growl rumbled out of his chest as he fought down the urge to shift before they both fell to the floor while they wrestled each other for control.

"Oi! No fighting in the bar! You boys calm down or take it outside!"

With a raised eyebrow, Dylan glanced over when he heard Trent hollering from the safety of behind the bar. With a long-suffering sigh, Ryan wrenched him away from Luke and Dylan staggered to his feet. Dylan had planned on letting it end there. He didn't want to get banned from the only pub that was anywhere near their home, but Luke obviously had other ideas. As soon as the bastard found his feet, he lunged at Dylan, hands outstretched and curled as if he had his lion claws out and ready to use. Was he planning on shifting in the middle of the bar?

"What the fuck? Cut the shit, Luke."

Ryan's voice was little more than a growl as he planted a hand on Luke's chest to keep him from reaching Dylan. Luke slapped Ryan's hand away and took a swing at him. Rage clouded Dylan's vision. No one messed with his twin. No one. With a growl, Dylan barreled straight into the stupid lion.

A low, hissing sound was the only warning before ice-cold water hit him in the back of the head. Dylan curled his lip as he spun around on his brother.

"What the fuck?"

Felines did not like their faces to get wet. Ever. Dylan took a menacing step toward his twin. His animal instincts on high alert, he seemed to be fighting off attacks from all angles. Ryan quickly dropped the hose and put his hands up as if he were surrendering.

"Easy, Dylan. It was the quickest way I could think of to get you two to quit laying into each other."

Dylan glanced over his shoulder to see Luke storming out the front door. Once more, he curled his lip with a growl as the bastard ran away. Typical. Always started the damn fight, never hung around for the ending. That's what happened to males who counted on their females to provide everything. Bloody lions and their "pride." Cheetah males looked after themselves, their mates and offspring. As it should be.

When Dylan spun back to give his twin a mouthful of abuse, his body began tingling. He froze and took a deep breath. There was a scent in the air, one he'd not smelled before but would know anywhere. He turned to Ryan, who was pulling the same shocked, silent routine as he was. Relief flowed through him. Their mother had been right when she assured him that he would share his mate with his twin.

"You smell it too?"

"Of course, I do. Wait, you doubted we'd share a mate?"

"I'd hoped we would share one but couldn't be certain. Fate can be twisted with its sense of humor."

Their mate was here in the pub. The thought hit him as his heart began to pound against his ribs. Since hitting puberty, Dylan had waited to smell that scent, and it was the sweetest moment of his life.

The flash of color as Trent tossed a towel had him snapping back to reality just in time to snatch it from mid air. Dylan wiped his face and hair with it before dropping it on the bar.

"Sorry, Trent. Didn't mean to start shit in the bar."

"Yeah, I know, mate. But you and Luke need to sort your shit out. You're not teenagers anymore."

Tell that to Luke, Dylan thought. Dropping all thoughts about the aggravating lion, he sat on the stool next to Ryan and casually turned to face away from the bar. He had much more pressing—and important—things to deal with. Like locating his mate.

"Where is she?"

"No idea. The air conditioning has her scent circulating around so I can't pinpoint it."

"We can't leave until we find her. Shit, my blood is pounding through my veins already."

"Mine, too. It's the Calling. Don't worry, Dylan. She'll be feeling something too. We'll find her."

Dylan took a deep breath as he rearranged himself on the stool. Damn, he hoped they found her tonight. His body was going to be strung tighter than a bow until they claimed her.

Lacey pressed her spine against the warm, worn leather of the booth, and her cheeks felt flushed as her mind raced a million miles a minute. That big guy had called the identical twins he'd been fighting with Ryan and Dylan.

Could they really be the guys that she'd been searching for? The two who had helped Cameron?

They certainly looked strong enough to climb down a cliff and rescue a small boy. She'd found herself mesmerized earlier when she caught sight of how their shoulder muscles bulged as they moved. Their tight, white t-shirts along with formfitting blue jeans disguised nothing about how sleek their physiques were.

Was that what they'd been fighting with that other man over? Cameron's rescue? She'd heard the loud one say something about getting the job done. That had been before they'd gotten into a fistfight, of course. Bloody men.

She wrapped her suddenly sweaty palms around her frosty drink, trying to calm her overheated body. She didn't know what was wrong with her, but her body having a major over-reaction to the pair of hot guys currently seated at the bar. Sure, they were handsome male specimens, but she'd seen good-looking men before and never had her lady bits throbbed with need in reaction. As she took a deep breath, she frowned. Did her nipples just harden with arousal beneath her bra and white tank top?

She couldn't resist finding out, and she moved to brush her palm surreptitiously against her breast, gasping as her sensitive nipple tightened further at the light caress.

What the hell? She wasn't even looking at them anymore!

As she twisted around, Lacey slowly straightened her spine and lifted her chin until she could see over the booth so the twins were in her line of vision once more. The tall man who'd been fighting with them was nowhere to be seen, and one twin was sitting while the other stood. Her heart rate skyrocketed, and her mouth went bone dry when they stopped talking and froze for a moment as if they sensed someone watching them. The man standing settled onto a stool, and she took a deep breath in relief, figuring she'd dodged a bullet. But before she could return to hiding in her booth, she saw both twins move on their stools to face away from the bar. When they lowered their heads and began scanning the room, she knew she was in trouble.

"Shit."

She ducked her head down and spun back around, grabbing the straw of her drink and sucking down the cold raspberry-flavored liquid.

"Hey, do you want another one?"

She made a slurping noise as she sucked the last drops from beneath the ice before she looked up to smile at the woman who was holding a round black tray while she chewed on some gum. Lacey tried not to stare, but it was hard not to when practically every bared inch of her flesh was covered in colorful tattoos.

"Um, no thanks, but I was wondering if I could ask you a question."

The woman snatched up a wet blue cloth off her tray and began wiping Lacey's table down, grabbing her empty glass as she did.

"Sure. Whatcha want to know?"

"Ah, those two guys at the bar, the twins..."

Miss Tattoos gave her a cheeky smile and struck a pose with her tray resting on a hip.

"Yeah, that's Dylan and Ryan. Their parents own the largest farm in the area, so everyone knows those boys. What about 'em?"

So, she'd overheard the names correctly earlier. Holy hell!

Heat flushed up her already warm cheeks as she made direct eye contact with the strange woman.

"I'm a reporter for the Melbourne Herald, and I'm following up a lead on a story. I was told Ryan and Dylan would be able to help me, but I don't think I should approach them here. Do you know where they work, or how I could contact them?"

The woman looked over at the bar, then back at Lacey, her shrewd blue gaze assessing Lacey's plain clothes and over-abundant breasts.

Lacey's spine stiffened under the waitress's scrutiny. The woman looked like a damn stick figure, and it made Lacey feel every pound she was carrying on her own curvy body. She fought the urge to lift her arms to cover her cleavage. Dammit, there was nothing wrong with her size eighteen body. She wasn't skinny, but she was fit and healthy and that's what mattered.

"They work at the open range zoo. Dylan's a chef in the restaurant out there, and Ryan's an animal keeper. As far as I know, they live on their parents' property."

They worked at the zoo? A little ironic that she was following a lead on men associated with cheetahs, only to find out that those men would have daily contact with the big, spotted cats.

"That's great. I'll call the zoo on Monday to speak with them. Thank you so much for your help."

The hair on the back of her neck had begun to tingle, and in a rush, Lacey grabbed her bag and looked towards the exit. She'd come out to the bar hoping to ask someone about the mysterious Ryan and Dylan. She hadn't expected to actually run into either of them, or to be turning tail and fleeing in the opposite direction as soon as she found what she'd been looking for. But until she could work out what was going on with her out of control hormones, she needed to retreat.

She hunched over, trying to make herself smaller as she snuck out of the booth. But she couldn't resist once last glance at the twins before she left. On a gasp, she nearly tripped when she saw both of their intense gazes were on her.

With a squeak, she moved faster, her heart pounding against her ribs. She shoved open the door and burst out into the warm night air, gulping oxygen into her burning lungs.

Oh, shit. They'd seen her checking them out.

Pull yourself together. With how good they looked, it wouldn't be the first time they'd had someone, especially a woman staring at them.

Just as she stepped from the concrete sidewalk onto the parking lot, something growled near her ear. Before she had time to react, a large hand gripped each of her hips and twisted her around so she was facing the side wall of the bar. Her handbag landed at her feet, and she raised her palms to push against the bricks to prevent her face slamming into the solid surface.

A sob caught in her throat as the man behind her pinned her body against the rough bricks with his and placed his hands over hers, lacing their fingers together.

Adrenaline was pumping through her system, making her heart pound and sweat bead on her forehead. She should have been fighting, screaming for help, but some perverse instinct inside her craved more contact. It made her want to push back against the strong body pinning her in place.

"Where you goin', beautiful?"

His voice was so deep that his words were barely more than a garbled growl, but she somehow understood what he'd said. The hairs on the back of her neck rose once more in response to the depth of possession that radiated from his tone.

"You're scaring her, Dylan. Cut it out."

Lacey panted as she looked toward the new voice. Ryan was gorgeous and sexy, but unlike his twin or her, he seemed to be considerably calmer and more in control.

"He's not scaring me." At least, not physically.

Strong desire, like she'd never experienced before, raced through her system. Just like in her favorite romance novels, it was instant, electric and all-consuming. Fire was in her blood, lighting her up from the inside out, centering in her pussy and taking root there.

Dylan nipped at her ear, and she moaned, letting her eyes slide shut as another, stronger, wave of arousal flowed through her. Her knees began to collapse on her, but before she could fall, a thick, muscular arm whipped around her waist and held her tight against a hard, hot body. Dylan's erection was now pressed into the cleft of her ass in a way that made her instinctively arch back into his embrace while whimpering a little.

"Shit. I'm sorry. Um, let's sit down."

Dylan seemed to be getting control of himself as he pulled her away from the wall and toward a nearby park bench.

Lacey moved as though in a daze. Everything looked a little hazy, like a light fog had moved in, and she kept stumbling over cracks in the concrete as she walked. The entire time they moved, Dylan kept a firm hold on her so at least she didn't fall and hurt herself while she was in whatever this daze was.

Once they reached the bench, Dylan released her, and she collapsed onto it. Both men moved to stand in front of her and she pressed her palms against the metal of the seat, allowing the coldness from the steel seep into her in the hope it would calm her mind. She was unable to process what she was seeing before her. Two sets of beautiful brown eyes, along with strong jaws and spiky black hair. A perfectly matched set. Squinting, she stared harder and saw smaller details. There were differences between them. One had a mole on the left side of his forehead and the other had one on the right.

"How much did you have to drink tonight?"

She laughed at the question, swaying with a delicious light-headedness that appeared to be caused by simply being close to these men.

"Ah, nothing other than one raspberry lemonade."

She giggled again then sobered with a frown, as she heard herself. She sounded like an idiotic teenager.

The men looked between each other, one flexing his fingers as though angry. Dylan maybe? She was fairly certain he was the one who'd grabbed her earlier but couldn't be sure. They were just so damn similar. Sensing something was off, Lacey's mind cleared somewhat, and she sat up straighter and focused more on the men in front of her. She needed to be smart about this and not let her hormones rule her in this moment.

"What's wrong with you now? One minute you're pinning me up against a wall, all hot and heavy, the next you're placating me, and now you look like you're ready to hit someone. Again."

The angry one, she thought was Dylan, stalked off with a harsh expletive while the other sat down on the seat next to her, a gentle smile on his lips.

"You saw Dylan fight with Luke?"

With her mind now clear, Lacey crossed her arms and nodded her head.

"Yeah, of course, I did. Everyone in the bar did. It was kind of funny seeing you finish it, though."

Ryan chuckled and cocked his head as he looked at her with an intensity that made butterflies take flight in her stomach. His eyes were flicking around her face as though studying her, a sexy smile playing on his full mouth.

Heat pooled between her thighs once more, and she bit her lip to stop herself from moaning. She felt like two different people who were fighting with each other. Part of her, an almost animalistic side, wanted to submit to these beautiful men and give them whatever they wanted, but the other, larger part of her, was questioning her sanity. She already had one psycho ex. She didn't need more weird men in her life.

Panic hit her as she realized she'd lost her clutch somewhere. "Where's my bag?"

She looked around, and Dylan, who was still lingering nearby, followed her gaze back to the side wall of the pub. He stomped over to pick up her black clutch from the ground before coming back to return to her, passing it over with jerky movements.

"I'm sorry."

"No need to be. I'm fine."

The words were out before she could even think them through.

She pressed her lips together and crossed her legs in front of her, trying her best to show herself to be a lady, despite all her previous actions – and thoughts – to the contrary.

"After everything that just happened, this feels a little ridiculous but let's go back to the start, shall we? I'm Lacey Clarke."

She smiled up at them and tried to ignore the stomach-gripping excitement that was building inside her. What was wrong with her?

"I'm Dylan Monaghan." The standing twin tapped himself on the chest and then pointed to his brother sitting beside her. "That's Ryan."

She smiled, unable to stop the inappropriate reaction to this bizarre situation.

"It's nice to meet you both. I've actually been looking for you. I'm a reporter with the Melbourne Herald, and I'm writing a story on the Cameron MacKenzie rescue. I have a few questions for you both."

CHAPTER FOUR

Ryan stopped breathing for a moment. A reporter? Their mate was a damn reporter for one of Melbourne's biggest newspapers? This couldn't be happening.

"What do we do, Ryan?"

"I have no fucking idea. But whatever it is, we need to be doing it away from here."

"Maybe if we claim her, she won't want to expose us?"

Ryan sighed out loud. They'd have to tell her the truth. Cheetahs were incapable of lying to their mates. Their minds simply couldn't process the concept of being dishonest to the one destined to complete them.

Lacey cleared her throat, sounding nervous, and Ryan realized he and Dylan had been silent for too long.

"That's a conversation that needs to happen behind closed doors."

He heaved out a breath as her eyes sparkled with interest.

"So, you'll talk to me? You'll answer my questions?"

He grimaced and looked away for a moment. He really didn't want to tell her anything, not until he was certain she was fully theirs. Maybe the lions had a point about all their rules...

"Come with us back to our place for dinner, and we'll discuss what happened last weekend."

Lacey's knuckles turned white as she gripped her clutch. Ryan frowned as he glanced from her hands up to her face. What was wrong with her? Her mouth was now pinched into a flat line, and she was squinting at him with an intensity he wasn't sure he liked.

"How do I know I can trust you both? I like meeting sources in public places, where I know I'm safe. How about a quiet restaurant? I'm not the kind of woman who makes it a habit to go home with men she's just met. No matter how interesting the information you have is."

Ryan inwardly cringed as his twin's face lit up with wide grin. Please don't let him say something that makes her run from us screaming.

"Well, that puts you in a pickle then, beautiful. Because there ain't a lot of options out here in the sticks. You can come back to our place with us now or wait until we can get away from work long enough to go into Melbourne. That wouldn't be until at least next weekend."

She sucked her full bottom lip into her mouth as she frowned. Ryan had to bite his tongue for a moment to stop himself from moaning. Her mouth was a lush little slice of heaven, and he wanted a taste of it so badly he ached.

He shook his head and searched for an alternative solution. But he struggled to think about anything other than claiming her as soon as possible.

"We live in a small house on our parents' farm. It's less than half a mile between our place and our folks', so you won't be completely alone with us out in the middle of nowhere. If you like, we could eat at the main house. You'd have to put up with at least some of our brothers, but our mother would be there too."

Her shoulders lowered a little and she loosened her death grip on her bag.

"Um, okay. I'll agree if we can do this at your parents' place. It's not too short notice for your mother?"

"I'll call to check, but she's always got plenty of food in the house, so I can't see it being an issue."

Not to mention the fact she'd be overjoyed that not only had her youngest sons found their mate, but she'd also get to meet her today.

"I'll call her now. Dylan? You'll stay with Lacey?"

"Of course."

"Don't do anything to scare her off before I get back."

"Yeah, yeah. I got this."

Ryan rolled his eyes at his twin's arrogant tone, rose from the seat and pulled his mobile free of his pocket as he walked a short distance away. While he hit the speed dial for home, he glanced back to see Dylan nervously sitting next to Lacey. He wasn't looking at her, instead tapping his fingers on his knee and glancing around. Ryan held back his laugh at seeing his normally overconfident, always-in-charge twin looking so lost at what to do. He hadn't strayed far when he heard the call connect.

"Hello, Ryan, what's up? Dylan didn't get into another fight, did he?"

Ryan grinned. Gotta love caller ID. His mother always knew who was calling now she had it.

"Well, he did, but that's not why I'm calling."

Her sigh came over the line like a strong gust of wind, long and forlorn. "Okay, I won't ask for any more details. I honestly don't want to know. So, what do you need me for? It's not like you or your brothers to ring home this late on a Friday afternoon."

"Um, Dylan and I wanted to bring someone around for dinner, and she'd be more comfortable at your place with a few more people around ... so, I just wanted to check if that's okay?"

"She? As in a woman?" His mother's voice was now high-pitched with excitement. Of course, she knew there was only one female he or Dylan would ever bring home to meet the family. "You've found your mate?"

He couldn't hold back the buzz that coursed through his blood or the pride in his voice as he answered. "That would be correct. She's a reporter with the Melbourne Herald and is doing a piece on the rescue. She wants to ask us some questions."

Ryan was being careful about what he said as he wasn't sure if Lacey could still hear him. He was a little way from her now but hadn't been able to force himself to go far enough to ensure she wasn't in earshot.

"What? Oh, hell. Okay, bring her over, and we'll do our best to help you sort this mess out. I'll go raid the fridge and see what I can come up with to add to what I've already got on the go."

"Who's at the house tonight?"

He hoped not everyone. He wasn't sure how Lacey would cope with all seven of their brothers plus them and their parents carrying on around the dinner table. It resembled a circus most times it happened. Fortunately, now they were all adults and had their own homes on the property, it didn't happen too often.

His mother chuckled. "You know full well once word gets out that your mate is coming to dinner, they'll all be here. She is Dylan's mate too?"

"Yeah, you were right about that."

"Okay, well you best get back to her and I'll see you all in a bit. Take your time coming out, though. Give me some time to prepare a full meal."

He could hear in her voice how excited she was and imagined as he hung up the phone that she was currently running around the house screaming her joy. Yeah, only one way all his family was going to find out about their dinner guest in the next half hour, and that was via his mother's big mouth.

"You've got to be kidding me."

Lacey's mouth gaped open as she put her car into park and turned off the engine. She reminded herself that she was only here to follow up a lead on the Cameron Mackenzie story, not to do a full review on the property, even though the beauty of her surroundings had her brain switching out of gear. This place was incredible!

She opened her door and got out as she stared up at the mansion that was Ryan and Dylan's family home.

"I know it looks a little overwhelming, but wait until you get inside. It's just like any other home. With so many kids, they needed a big house. I love how my parents built the place on the highest point of the property so that they could oversee the entire place."

"Sorry?" Lacey hadn't been paying attention as she was still mesmerized by the sash windows, massive wraparound porch and the sheer grandeur of the sprawling, single story homestead.

"Look." Ryan, or she assumed he was Ryan, due to his calm aura and gentle voice, turned her around so that she now looked away from the house and back toward the direction they had driven in. She let out another contented sigh, her shoulders dropping down as though a weight had been lifted off them.

"Wow." The house was on the top of a rise that had resulted in a breathtaking view that extended for several miles in all directions, which including several other homes that she assumed were their children's houses. "So, they still look after you guys huh?"

Ryan shrugged and grinned. "They're pretty awesome parents."

Tears prickled at the back of Lacey's eyes and a lump formed in her throat, so she coughed to clear it as she blinked rapidly. What was it about a man who loved his parents that got to her so much? Probably due to the fact that she had such a distant relationship with her own family and the one thing she'd always longed for was the closeness that she could see these men shared with their relatives.

"So, how old are you two, anyway?"

What made her ask that, she had no idea. It certainly wasn't pertinent to the story.

"Twenty-three." Ryan grinned, and Dylan sauntered up, knocking his twin's shoulder roughly with his own. "But I'm older."

Ryan shoved him back with a quick reflex. "Yeah, by a whole three minutes."

Lacey laughed. She couldn't help it. As an only child with her sort of parents, sibling camaraderie was another thing she had no experience with.

"Cool."

She stared at the men before her as her mind began to catalogue the differences between them. Dylan's face was slightly longer, Ryan's a bit rounder. Dylan's lips were curved into a cheeky smile, which flashed the dimple in his left cheek, and his gorgeous brown eyes were bright with humor. Ryan seemed to always be more reserved, more serious, even in his looks. She wondered if he'd have a dimple in his right cheek...

"Hello, boys," a strong woman's voice called out. When the twins turned toward her, they spun in opposite directions, and Lacey couldn't help but chuckle. She glanced up and saw who must be their mother standing on the front porch, a serene smile on her face and white apron in place.

Ryan took Lacey's hand in his, and surprised by his touch, she tried unsuccessfully to pull free. For some strange reason, within seconds the warmth of his skin and the feel of his callused palm touching hers settled her. The waitress had said Ryan was an animal keeper, so he must be like a horse whisperer, assuming animals reacted to him like she just had.

They began walking up to the house and Lacey's stomach did a nervous little flip, like this was a first date or something, and not the purely professional interview that it was meant to be.

Yeah, but the last few hours haven't exactly been normal, have they?

"Hello, I'm Maggie Monaghan."

Lacey was a little awestruck. Maggie was simply beautiful. Everything a mother should be. Her warmth glowed around her like that white ring that surrounds the moon on special nights. It was in her aura, every line of her face, and the naturally dark brown hair that was shot through with grey.

Her cheeks heated as she realized she'd been standing there silent, staring like a fool.

"Mum, this is Lacey."

Her eyes widened in surprise as Dylan had spoken. His voice had dropped to such a low level she could only describe it as gravelly. And it made her body tingle in an extremely unprofessional way. What the hell was with that?

He shot her a sideways glance but offered her no explanation.

"It's lovely to meet you, Lacey. Please, won't you come in?"

Maggie waved her in, and Lacey ascended the stairs. Ryan finally released her hand, and she clenched it onto her bag as her nervousness resurfaced. Maybe this wasn't such a good idea. She had the strangest feeling that once she entered this home, she'd never be the same again.

She followed Maggie, who she noticed was nicely rounded like herself, through the front door and was instantly hit by a cacophony of noise. It reminded her of when she'd step out into a hot summer's day, after being in the cold air-conditioned office all day. A harsh shock to her system that stole her breath and stilled her mind.

After forcing her feet to move two steps into the house, she couldn't go any further. The delicious smell of roasted meat and potatoes combined with a raucous amount of laughter and the voices of several men talking. This wasn't what she'd had in mind. She envisioned one or two brothers, not an army of them! This was worse than meeting the twins alone somewhere.

"It's okay, it's just our brothers."

Ryan's statement wasn't reassuring in the least.

"And how many are there?"

Lacey couldn't make her feet move, firmly caught between her fight or flight instincts. Did she stay or did she run while she still could?

"This was meant to be just an interview. I think I've made a mistake."

She began backing towards the door, her heart pounding against her ribs as her feet shuffled on the polished wood floor.

As both twins lunged toward her, they both made strange growling noises in their throats that caused her skin to tingle, but it was Maggie that reached her first. The older woman slid her arm around Lacey's shoulders and gently began to lead her toward the noise.

She chuckled as she squeezed Lacey's arm. "Don't you worry about a thing, sweetheart. You'll get your interview, and you can sit with me if you like. It'll be nice to have a little more estrogen around here for once."

Lacey's panicking calmed instantly as Maggie's gentle touch and smooth voice washed over her. Just like Ryan's touch had done earlier.

"I only came to ask a few questions about Cameron Mackenzie."

Maggie chuckled again. "Oh, that's a great story. It has cheetahs and everything. You have to stay so you can hear it all."

"I knew it! He wasn't lying."

Excitement chased away her previous fears until they stepped through a pair of wooden double doors and the loud chorus of deep male voices ceased as though they were on a switch. Flick, then silence.

Eight sets of golden-brown eyes stared at her, all of them belonging to beautiful men.

Lacey's knees went weak, and Maggie squeezed her tightly as she sagged, leaning in to whisper, "Chin up, love, and you'll soon be running rings around all of them."

Maggie lifted her head and continued to drag Lacey toward the large dining room table.

"Everyone, this is Lacey. Lacey, my other seven sons and my husband, Brad Monaghan."

Nine sons? Holy shit! As an only child this was so far out of her realm of normal, she couldn't begin to process it. The older man, the father, stood at the other end of the table before he walked around to them, his brown eyes twinkling with mischief much like Dylan's had earlier.

"You look like Dylan," she blurted out, and there was a moment of silence before everyone in the room burst into laughter.

"I sure hope so, Lacey. He is my boy." Brad's chuckle was deep and strong, exactly what Lacey had always assumed an Alpha male would sound like.

"C'mon, boys, sit down." Maggie fluttered her hands at her sons, and all nine of them fell into line, or more accurately, into their chairs.

"It's lovely to meet you, Lacey, and welcome to our home." Brad Monaghan nodded at her and headed back to his own seat.

"Sit here, Lacey." Maggie once again tugged her into a chair and indicated to the delicious fare before them. "Don't be shy now, dig in."

The men didn't need to be told twice, all ten of them grabbing at the various bowls of different types of salads, forking pieces of cooked meat and sharing around bread and drinks while sliding curious sideways glances at her.

"Here you go." Ryan exchanged his extremely full plate with her empty one and began filling it. "You'll miss out if you don't hurry."

"Thanks." Lacey picked up her fork and ignored the interested looks from all of Dylan and Ryan's brothers. She'd never be able to eat all Ryan had served her, but she'd try to put a reasonable sized dent in it at least. She scanned around the table. They were all well-built, tall and handsome. They were a lethal combination for any woman with red blood pulsing in her veins.

CHAPTER FIVE

Lacey began eating the wholesome, delicious food, between answering the few questions Maggie sent her way. The conversation stayed light, for which Lacey was grateful. At least, until she'd eaten all she could and was about to set her cutlery down. It was then that one of the brothers, a rather cheeky one, looked her way.

"So, Mum says you're a journalist."

She nodded, heat flaming in her cheeks as every person at the table turned their full attention her way.

"And you're looking into what happened with that kid Dylan and Ryan saved?"

She nodded again, her whole body quivering with nerves. "So, it's true that the twins rescued him?"

The smug brother gave her a sexy smirk. "Hell, yeah. Of course, it's true. It sure as fuck wasn't the lions. There's no one else around here that can move the way we do."

"Max! Language at the table! Don't think I won't wash your mouth out with soap just because you're grown."

"Sorry, Mum."

As entertaining as it was to watch a fully grown man cower at his mother's threat of a forced soap mouth wash, Lacey was stuck on how the men saved the boy while appearing to him as animals. And who'd mentioned anything about freaking lions? Cameron had said cheetahs...

"And what are you guys exactly?"

"Max, I don't think that's your place..." Maggie tried to interrupt again, but this time Max simply continued on over her.

"We're cheetahs, baby. Fastest and most agile of all the big cats."

Lacey swallowed hard as a ringing started in her ears. She'd heard this from Cameron but hadn't thought it actually possible. She decided that false bravado was the best tact with this particular brother. She was going to fake it till she made it. Especially since no one else was jumping up to help out. The room had gone deathly quiet.

"Really? Well, Cameron did tell me he was rescued by a couple of cheetahs, but I hadn't thought it was truly possible. Did a couple escape from the zoo or something, and this is all a cover-up for it?"

She looked around the group of now shuffling, uncomfortable-looking males when Ryan reached over and put his hand over hers. "No, wild cheetahs would have hurt the boy. Sweetheart, Max is telling you the truth. We're shifters, more specifically cheetah shape shifters. We can turn into our feline form anytime we need or want to."

Lacey's chest felt tight, and her lungs wouldn't work right. She forced out a laugh, then coughed a little to clear her dry throat. Fake it till you make it. She kept repeating the mantra in her mind.

"Really? I'd like to see that."

And that was all it took for all seven brothers to push their chairs back and stand up.

Max rushed to the door, "Awesome! Let's go show her before she changes her mind."

"May as well get it over and done with," she heard one of them mutter as they walked past her and out the door toward the front of the house.

Completely overwhelmed, she turned away from the huge men as she attempted to calm her breathing.

She searched out the twins with her gaze, finding first Dylan then Ryan. Their eyes sparkled with excitement while Dylan's jaw was set hard, and Ryan's mouth was turned down a little.

"Where are they all going?"

"Uh..."

Maggie stood up and motioned to the twins to head out the room. "Looks like this is happening regardless of your plans, boys. You two may as well join your brothers. Lacey, this is going to be one hell of a show that you'll never forget."

She looked straight at Lacey and smiled gently. "I hope you're ready for this, Lacey."

Acid burned in the back of her throat, but she managed to push herself to her shaky feet.

"What am I really about to see, Maggie?"

She walked next to the shorter woman, her muscles quivering in anticipation of what was to come.

"The other side of my family."

When Maggie pushed open the entrance door to reveal the front porch, Lacey's hand flew to cover her mouth as she gasped in shock. Ten large spotted cats sat or prowled around the space before her. They all had the cheetah's iconic black tearstain lines on their faces along with lithe, agile, feline bodies.

Lacey choked on a scream as her lungs froze in her chest. She jerked back, and her heart began to pound so fast it was all she could hear.

"No. This can't be."

She struggled to speak with her dry mouth and her tongue refusing to work right. One of the cats purred and stepped forward, making direct eye contact with her. She gasped again in horror as she recognized the gaze as Dylan's—just with more gold and less brown than his human irises. She stumbled backwards and landed hard against the doorframe, pain splintering through her shoulder as black spots formed before her and grew until they eclipsed her vision.

"No..." Her whisper was hoarse as she struggled to get air into her lungs. I can't breathe!

Maggie cried out as Lacey felt her body loosen and begin to fall. The world turned on its axis, and she heard a tortured, animalistic whine as everything went pitch black.

Panicked, Dylan shifted back to human and clothed himself in a pair of jeans as he dove to catch his mate. His knees hit the rough timber of the deck hard but he ignored the sharp, jarring pain that ran up his thighs as Lacey landed limply in his lap. Phew. He'd gotten to her in time. Not wasting a moment, he brushed the dark strands of hair away from her pale face and neck so he could find her pulse point. Pressing two fingers against her throat, he held his breath until he felt what he was searching for, the steady beating of her heart. His shoulders sagged with relief.

"She's alive, Ryan, she's alive."

"Thank fuck for that!"

Squeezing his eyes closed he cradled her against his chest for a moment, sensing Ryan kneeling on the other side of Lacey. Without a word, he knew his brother needed to reassure himself that she was okay, that she'd merely fainted. Dylan pressed a kiss to Lacey's clammy forehead before he gently handed her over to his twin. The moment she was safe in his brother's embrace, he stood and whirled around on a growl.

"Max, you had no right! Lacey is our mate, not yours. It was our decision on when and how we would tell her our truth!"

He took a menacing step toward his arrogant brother, who, like all of his siblings, was now in human form. He would pay, in flesh, for harming his mate.

"Dylan! Stop!"

His father's booming voice cut through the night air like a whip, and a primal instinct took over Dylan's body and rendered him motionless. That was the voice of his Alpha. It was a tone that no cheetah in their coalition could disobey and one his father very rarely used.

"Max was impulsive with his decision to speak and act as he did tonight, and he will receive punishment. But that punishment will not be by your hand, son. I will not stand for my children fighting with such violence as you intend to inflict on your brother, Dylan. You and Ryan shifted along with all of your brothers. None of you are blameless. Go with Ryan and take your mate home and care for her, knowing that I will handle Max. Neither you nor Ryan will seek any further justice in regard to the matter."

Dylan whined a little, but he bowed slightly to his father. His blood still boiled and needed an outlet, but he would not go against his father's orders. Especially since his father was right. He or Ryan could have stood up to Max before they all shifted. Dammit, he was so used to following his older siblings' lead. But none of them were mated. He and Ryan were the first to find their mate, so they were all in completely uncharted territory. This was going to be up to him and Ryan to work out. He needed to remember that and not allow his brothers to put stupid ideas in his head. He moved to follow Ryan down the steps to their car where he opened the door for Ryan to climb in with their mate, his heart still racing and his throat dry.

He closed his twin and their mate safely in before moving around the front of the car to the driver's door. Just before he opened it, he took a deep breath, paused and looked up to the house. His fury had dampened a little, and he was grateful his father had stepped in. He didn't want to hurt any of his family. He loved each one of them. He could see now he hadn't really been mad at Max, but rather the situation. He would have never forgiven himself if he'd permanently maimed any of his brothers like he'd intended to do to Max. With a heavy sigh, he opened the door but froze as he heard his father's voice echoing out from the house.

"Max, you will spend a full ten days in cheetah form in the feeding yard at the zoo. That should give you ample time to consider your actions, and next time you want to come between a cheetah and his mate, you will think twice before you do it. You should have at least discussed revealing our truth to Lacey with the twins before you went ahead and did it."

A shudder ran through Dylan as he slid into the car and drove toward their home. That was harsh. The feeding yard was what they called the smaller enclosure at the zoo where they kept a pair of cheetahs that were feed twice daily near a platform people could come and watch from. Normally, the shifters never went in there. There wasn't room to run at full speed and having people oohing and ahhing over them while they ate was downright degrading. Maybe he should have just knocked Max out. It would have been kinder to him. Dylan grinned as he guessed his brother was probably wishing for the same thing about now. He eyed his twin and their mate.

"How's she doing?"

"Hasn't stirred yet, but her breathing has evened out, and her skin isn't cold anymore."

That was good. Dylan let the comfortable silence linger as he drove. In a matter of minutes, Dylan pulled up in front of their house and moved around to open the way for Ryan. Dylan took her from his twin and couldn't believe how right she felt in his arms. With Ryan's help, he got her inside and before long they had Lacey settled on Ryan's bed.

Dylan stepped away and let his brother take over, standing in the doorway with his arms folded over his chest as Ryan gently removed her shoes. He sucked at this stuff.

"What do we do now, Ry?"

Ryan shrugged as he moved to stand next to him.

"Guess we just have to wait for her to wake up. She got one hell of a shock. Thankfully, you caught her before she injured herself, so hopefully she'll wake up soon."

He nodded at his brother and sent up a prayer of thanks to his father, grateful for the inherited ability for fast shifting he'd been born with.

"Okay. And what the hell do we do with her when she wakes up?"

Ryan rubbed the bridge of his nose. "We need to work out a way to keep her here with us. I was hoping we could make at least a little headway with her before we told her about our truth, but that plan's been blown out of the water."

Dylan growled as his anger rose again.

"If she runs from us and refuses to see us ever again, I'm going to make Max's life hell. Regardless of what Dad said."

Ryan sighed. "You don't mean that, and you know it. We're as much to blame as Max. We didn't have to blindly follow his lead to shift in front of her. How about you go for a run back to the house and bring her car down here?"

He eyed off his sleeping mate, heat stirring in his groin at how beautiful she was lying on the dark blue comforter Ryan kept on his bed. Lacey showed no sign of stirring yet, so he supposed he did have time to do what Ryan had suggested.

"Go on, I won't leave her side. And if she wakes up to find you in this mood, it's not going to help our cause."

With a snarl, Dylan tilted his head until his neck cracked. Stress set off his fight or flight mechanism every time, and man, was he in the mood for a fight. His twin had a point.

"Okay, okay. I'll go."

He forced himself from the room then the house, which was difficult. His instincts demanded he stay close to his mate, but Ryan was right. He needed to cool off, and Lacey would want her car and belongings close by. Had she brought her handbag into the house with her before dinner? He hoped not. He really didn't want to have to risk running into anyone tonight. They'd want to talk, but with the mood he was in, he'd be more likely to rip their heads off. He valued his family too much to risk that happening.

Standing in front of their home, he took a deep breath and looked up at the half moon in the clear, country sky. He closed his eyes and called on his magic to strip his clothes and transform him to his feline form.

The moment his four feet hit the ground, he took off at a sprint up to the main house. There was nothing faster than a cheetah going flat out, and he made the distance in no time. He circled her car twice before finally stopping and shifting back to human, his muscles quivering from the run. A delicious feeling of adrenaline pumping through him settled his anger down to a manageable level. He glanced into the car and saw her bag on the driver's seat. As he opened the door, he smelled his mother's scent and knew she'd placed Lacey's things out here for them.

He smiled as he opened her purse to look for her keys. His mother seriously rocked. He fumbled around in her bag for a moment before guilt had him clenching his jaw. His mother had taught him better than to rifle through a woman's handbag uninvited. Just as he palmed her key chain, the screen on her phone lit up with a text message. He pulled the phone out to check who it was. Afternoon had turned to evening, and Dylan wasn't sure if Lacey lived with her parents or a friend who would be worried about her not having returned yet.

The caller ID flashed up "Dead Horse," and he chuckled. He guessed it wasn't her housemate or parents. Curiosity got the better of him. He was a cat, after all, and he opened the message to see what this Dead Horse had to say.

Where r u? U should b home by now. U betta not b with a man. Ur mine.

A primal roar built up inside him, but he tamped it down as his mind spun with possibilities. Did Lacey have a boyfriend? They hadn't asked her. Although, considering what she'd saved the guy's name as in her contact list, he doubted they were involved. Maybe he was an ex that wasn't moving on? A psycho—a possessive one by the looks of that message.

His father's voice filled his mind. "You're flogging a dead horse, son." They'd been trying to get the old tractor to start, but it had died for good. His dad had been right that it was a waste of Dylan's time, but he'd enjoyed mucking around with it, trying to get it to work.

He jumped in the car and gunned the engine before he raced back to his house. He needed to tell Ryan about this, and if it turned out Lacey had a stalker ... well, they had some planning to do.

CHAPTER SIX

Soft evening light flitted in front of Lacey's eyes as she began to wake up. She took a deep breath and stretched her achy arms above her head until a jolt of pain came from her shoulder. Frowning, she tried to remember what the hell had happened. When did she fall asleep? She couldn't remember even lying down.

Searching her mind for answers, she noticed how warm and safe she felt. It had been so long since she had experienced anything other than gut-wrenching fear and loneliness, she'd nearly forgotten what it was like without those emotions dominating her mind. Mentally shrugging, she concluded it didn't matter why. She was going to focus on enjoying the sensation for as long as it lasted instead of analyzing it. Not even the pain in her shoulder was enough to lessen the peace she felt.

"Hmmm." She smiled as she hummed a little, relishing her newfound peace until she opened her eyes fully and they focused on a strange fan slowly turning above her. She'd never seen that modern, silver light-fan combo before. Panic froze her lungs for a moment as she turned her head from side to side, the swishing sound of her hair against the sheets loud in her ears. Where the fuck was she?

She sat up so fast her vision dimmed for a moment, her heart pounding like a bass drum as she gripped handfuls of the coverlet to steady herself.

"Lacey, it's okay. You're safe."

She gasped as she spun around to face one of the twins.

"Which one are you?" Her voice sounded shrill as she scrambled off the large bed, her eyes darting around the room and cataloguing more details as she pressed her spine against the cool wall. It was a large bedroom. Several photos and other trinkets lay scattered around on the tops of the furniture. The colors were masculine and the room neat. It had to be his room. Which one was he? She turned her focus back onto the dark-haired man who now stood way too close to her. He took a step back, holding his hands up to placate her.

"I'm Ryan. Dylan will be back any minute. He just went up to the main house to retrieve your car for you."

Main house? So where was she now? Lacey took short, quick breaths, swallowing several times in an attempt to wet her suddenly dry throat. She barely knew these guys. They could have done anything to her while she was asleep.

She glanced down and took note of her clothes. Her jeans were still on, buttoned and undamaged. Her blouse was only a little ruffled, which could have easily happened as she'd slept, and she seemed to be untouched. She did a quick internal log of her body and found no pain or injury. What had happened? She begged her memory to get with the program and help her out as she looked back toward Ryan.

"Ah, yes, of course. Sorry, Ryan."

She had cause to feel alarmed, she knew, but the poor guy looked really hurt that she'd forgotten who he was. She hadn't felt unsafe once with them, so why was she freaking out now?

Because I have a habit of attracting psychos!

She grimaced at the truth in her thoughts and focused back on the man in front of her. Gorgeous brown eyes, spiky dark hair. Now she'd calmed down, she could see it was him by his cool aura, the slightly rounder face and the mole.

He smiled gently, dropping his hands down and letting them fall to his sides.

"It's okay. Some of the people who have known us since birth still mix Dylan and me up."

Lacey took a few steps towards a framed photo of the twins, trying to focus on something normal. She smiled at the silly shot of the brothers out camping somewhere before she moved back toward the bed, concentrating on slowing her breathing so she didn't pass out again. Which, considering her current situation, was what had obviously happened. It was really the only logical conclusion.

"I know it's you, Ryan. I was just a little freaked out for a bit when I woke, so didn't look at you close enough before I spoke."

She continued pacing, the memory of huge cats coming back to haunt her. Had she dreamt that? She must have, as that couldn't have possibly been real.

"How did you know, Lacey?"

"Huh?" She glanced back at Ryan, who was watching her from where he now sat on the edge of the bed. His warm, calm aura reached out to her, soothing her frayed nerves. Damn, he really was a gorgeous man.

"How did you know it was me, not Dylan?"

She took a deep breath and let the air out slowly. "You feel different from Dylan. Warmer, calmer, softer. Your face is different too. Rounder, more serious. And the mole ... you know."

She shrugged as she flapped her hands, still feeling a little strange.

A door slammed and she jumped on a gasp, her ribs tightening so it made it difficult to breathe.

Ryan rose to his feet and made his way to the closed wooden door and opened it slowly.

"Take it easy, Lacey. It's just Dylan."

And like Ryan's words had conjured him, he appeared in the doorway, the harsher face and aura as easy to see now as the mole on the left side of his face.

He turned towards her, his eyes burning with something intense before he frowned in concern. "You're awake at last. You feeling all right?"

She nodded her head, tears swimming in her eyes at his question. Why did they seem to genuinely care about her? They'd only meet mere hours ago. What sort of trick was this?

She gulped and focused on keeping her voice at a normal pitch when she answered. "Yeah, I'm fine. I was just wondering why on earth I remember seeing cheetahs at your parents' place. Or did I dream that?"

The twins looked at each other with an intense focus, and Lacey wondered how it would feel to be stared at in such a way. She examined their faces more closely. Were they communicating silently with each other?

"Are you guys doing some special twin mind-meld thing?"

She'd heard stories about twins who could communicate telepathically and feel each other's extreme emotions.

Dylan turned toward her and his harsh frown melting into a broad grin, and a cheeky glint forming in his eyes. Her traitorous body turned into a bowl of goo in less than a heartbeat. Dylan was a devastatingly handsome man.

"You got it in one, beautiful. Ryan and I can speak into each other's minds."

"Okay." She shrugged and collapsed into a chair by the window, looking out as the last of the sun's rays sank down over the horizon. It really was beautiful out here on their farm.

"Uh, Lacey?" It was Ryan, she could tell by the tone alone.

"Yes, Ryan?" she asked without looking back at them.

There was a heavy silence for a moment. Then she felt his heat as he moved closer to her. His strong fingers under her chin forced her to turn her head to look at them.

"Do you remember us telling you about the cheetahs? About our family?"

Lacey frowned, lifting her face away from his touch as her mind dragging up the memory like it was a dusty old file being pulled out of an archive.

She cocked her head as her mind finally recalled what had happened earlier. A gasp escaped her throat as images flickered through her mind. Everything she'd learned came rushing back to her like a tidal wave, crashing over her and overwhelming her once again.

"Oh. My. Gosh." She had to get away from here. Lacey pushed herself to her feet and with her arms wrapped around her waist, she began backing towards the door, never taking her eyes off the men in front of her. The cheetahs, they were men. Men who could turn into wild cats. Their brothers... them ... oh shit!

"You. You're..." She shook her head as she struggled to remember what they'd called themselves.

"Don't be afraid of us, we'd never hurt you. We're cheetah shifters, Lacey, and we have a lot to discuss." Ryan spoke to her with his smooth voice that calmed her in a strange way—and confused the hell out of her. He made her want to stay and talk to them when she knew she should be running for the hills.

"About what?"

Ryan opened his mouth, but nothing came out. Lacey waited and watched as his eyes went wide and then he finally shut his mouth again. She was almost at the door, and the boys were still standing by the window.

Dylan groaned from his place beside Ryan, crossed his arms over his chest and rolled his eyes with exaggerated impatience.

"About the fact that you're our mate and we need you to stay with us."

"Geeze, Dylan. Just drop it like a bomb, why don't you? I was trying to figure out how to say it in a way that wouldn't freak her out."

"Brother, there was no way to do that, and you know it."

Lacey's jaw dropped open as she froze in place just by the door. As the twins continued to bicker with each other, her brain repeated what Dylan had said and tried to find a way to make it make sense.

"Your ... mate?" Like an animal's mate? And Dylan had said "our" not "my." They couldn't possibly be serious.

Instantly, they stopped talking and faced her. In unison, they nodded their heads like they were two mechanical dolls. Lacey glared at them while her hands clenched into fists at her sides.

"You cannot be fucking serious. First you tell me that you're some sort of freakish cat people and now that I'm your mate. Like your soul mate? What the hell does that even mean?"

Dylan stared back, his chocolate eyes a perfect complement to his dark hair.

"It means that you're meant for us, that you will complete our family. We're meant to love you, look after you and make sure you have everything you need to be happy for the rest of our lives."

Lacey laughed, and the uncontrolled sound was harsh and loud in the quiet room. When her ears rang from the noise, she put a hand over her mouth to muffle it, but she couldn't seem to stop. Had she lost her mind? Gone mad and was now imagining things? Two tears slipped down her cheeks at the ridiculousness of her evening.

It was a few minutes before she could control herself enough to be able to speak.

"Just great. And I suppose all those 'ours,' 'we' and 'us' you keep saying are you telling me we're destined to have some freaky ménage a trois for the rest of our lives? Oh, yeah, because that's totally normal and makes perfect fucking sense."

Another round of laughter bubbled up out of her and she couldn't stop it, not even when her sides began to ache, and her throat burned. As if she could be a mate to anyone, let alone two gorgeous men. Fear tickled up her spine as she realized she may well have truly lost her mind. That or these men were playing one hell of a nasty trick on her.

"Ry, what's wrong with her? Why's she laughing like a maniac?"

Ryan frowned as he watched Lacey. Her face had paled as she'd continued to laugh in a slightly hysterical manner.

"I don't think she believes us."

"She must feel the connection between us. Maybe we should kiss her?"

Ryan frowned as he considered his twin's suggestion. Why not? It couldn't do any harm, and her meltdown was breaking his heart. Ryan never wanted to see his mate like this ever again.

"Okay, c'mon then. I hate seeing her this upset."

"Only a woman would manage to laugh and cry at the same time."

Ignoring Dylan's last remark, Ryan moved to approach her from the right, while Dylan moved in from the left. As gently as he could, Ryan cupped her face in his palms. She made an adorable squeaking sound in surprise as her eyes flew open. They were a little unfocused, and her breathing was heavy as she finally stopped laughing. Using his thumbs, he wiped the tears from her cheeks.

"We're speaking the truth, Lacey. Please believe us."

He tilted her head up to him as he lowered his lips toward hers. Relief washed through him when she didn't pull from his grip as he got close enough to see the flecks of green in her hazel irises. His gaze roamed over her face, taking in her high cheekbones and perfectly sculpted eyebrows. She had a light layer of makeup on her skin, and when he was this close, he could see a few freckles beneath it. He heard the hitch in her breath over the sound of his blood pounding in his ears a moment before his mouth finally connected with hers.

Ryan groaned as sparks of awareness tingled across every inch of his flesh. If there had been any doubt she was his, it just evaporated. His cheetah wanted to purr in delight. Lacey opened her mouth beneath his on a moan, and he took the invitation and danced his tongue with hers.

He actually did purr when he felt her hands smooth up the front of his shirt until she wound her arms around his neck. When her fingers dove into his hair, Ryan got serious and tilted his head to deepen the kiss. He could do this forever. He'd never get enough of Lacey's sweet taste.

Ryan felt Dylan move up against Lacey's back and unfortunately wasn't surprised when she tensed as her large, soft breasts pressed into him from his twin's weight. On a shocked gasp, she tore free from his mouth and moved her hands back to his chest where she shoved him. Hard.

"What the hell are you two doing to me? I can't … I can't do this."

An ache started in Ryan's chest and with a grimace, he stepped away from his mate, her flushed red face making him feel like a bastard.

"I was trying to help you. We don't like seeing you upset, beautiful."

"What? So you thought you could kiss it better? Like I'm a five-year-old with a skinned knee?"

Ryan winced at her rather apt description, but before he could speak, Dylan jumped in.

"Hell, yeah, we thought we'd kiss it better. It's got nothing to do with how old you are, and I didn't get my turn. Ryan, we need to remember she needs a kiss from both of us in the future, or it doesn't work right. She's still upset."

With a sigh, Ryan watched Lacey narrow her eyes at his twin. Dylan's humor took some getting used to and clearly, now was not the time to start getting Lacey accustomed to it.

"Dylan, cut the jokes. Now is not the time."

"Who's joking? I didn't get a kiss. You got one. Totally unfair."

Lacey was rubbing her face in her hands now as she made a groaning noise.

"I can't date two men at once! It's insane. And I'm not mating anyone. So, you both can get over that idea right now."

"Oh, baby, we're gonna love proving you wrong."

Ryan thumped his brother on the arm. "Wait, would ya? Lacey, why can't you date us? Have you got a boyfriend already?"

He felt his brother stiffen, and anger radiated off him in waves. Ryan glanced at him, thinking Dylan's response a little excessive in his opinion.

"What the fuck is your issue, Dylan?"

"I just remembered the text I saw on her phone. Somebody wanted to know why she didn't go home. She had him saved under 'Dead Horse.'"

Ryan groaned. Great. He didn't want to go through a possessive human to get to his mate.

"I don't have a boyfriend. And quit doing the twin mind-meld thing in front of me. It's rude."

A grin spread over Ryan's face. Lacey had her arms crossed beneath her breasts and was looking a little fierce. Which on her was totally adorable.

"Dylan was just telling me about how your phone chirped while he was driving your car here earlier with a text from 'Dead Horse.' He's worried we have some competition for your attention."

As her face drained of color, Ryan inwardly cursed. She glared hard at Dylan. "You had no right to invade my privacy like that! How dare you go anywhere near my phone!"

❖ ❖ ❖ ❖ ❖

Dylan raised his hands up in surrender as she turned her fury on him. She was cute when she got worked up, but he didn't want her thinking he'd gone snooping when he hadn't. Not on purpose, anyway.

"I was looking for your keys when the screen lit up. I wasn't sure if you lived with your folks or a housemate, so I had a quick look to see if it was someone worried about you not being home yet. I'm guessing Dead Horse isn't your housemate?"

"No. He's a stupid ex that doesn't know when to quit. I hate to think what the message said. Please tell me you didn't read it?"

Dylan's cheeks heated, an uncomfortable and almost foreign feeling to him.

"Uh, like I said, I thought it might be someone you live with. I didn't want them to worry about you, so yeah, I saw the message."

Lacey stomped up to him and poked him in the chest with a finger. "How dare you! Is privacy a foreign concept? Gah, this is so embarrassing. I'm leaving. This is just all too much."

Panic had him grabbing for her, pulling her stiff body in against his.

"I'm sorry, Lacey. I honestly did it out of concern, and for no other reason. Please stay a while and talk with us."

Damn, she felt good in his embrace. Soft, warm, and downright sexy. The desire to kiss her full, red mouth was almost overwhelming, but he knew she wouldn't welcome it yet. Her shoulders slumped and she rested her forehead against his chest. He wrapped his arms tighter around her, the need to keep her close as natural as breathing. She was such a little thing, their mate. She inhaled deeply before she shuddered a little against him. When she pushed herself away from him, he reluctantly released her. He bit his tongue to stop himself speaking as she turned and left the bedroom in silence. He passed a worried glance at his twin before following her. Ryan didn't look like he had any idea what to do either.

Dylan found Lacey opening cupboards in the kitchen.

"What are you looking for?"

"I just wanted a glass of water."

Kicking himself for not already asking if she was thirsty after she'd passed out like she had, he rushed to her side.

"Here, let me get it for you."

She stiffened like she was going to argue, but in the end moved from the cupboards. As he pulled down a glass and filled it with fresh water, he could feel her gaze on him. What was she thinking? He took the drink over to her and caressed his fingers over hers as she took it from him. He swallowed the groan that rose and suppressed the smile that tugged at his lips. His skin tingled where it had touched her, confirming beyond a shadow of a doubt she was his mate.

"So, what is the real reason you put the brakes on things in the bedroom? Was it me?"

Lacey sputtered water down her chin as she coughed.

Dylan had never been one to mince words or put off the inevitable. They needed to deal with Lacey's doubts, and fast. His body ached for his mate, and he could feel Ryan suffering the same way he was.

"Damn, you don't beat around the bush, do you?"

He shrugged as his gaze followed her fingers while they wiped the water from her skin. He wanted to touch her there, kiss and caress every inch of her luscious body.

"Well, I've already mentioned how I feel about dating two men. And even if that wasn't an issue, I'm not the kind of woman who falls into bed with a man on the first date. Which this wasn't supposed to be. It was meant to be a causal dinner where I asked you both questions for my story."

Dylan grimaced, noting the angry glint in her eye and the accusatory tone in her voice. "Yeah, well, your questions got answered. But I really wish you wouldn't put them in your story. The last thing we need is to be outed to the general public. It would make our lives really difficult, and there would be no way we could stay here. Our whole family would have to move."

Lacey sat on a barstool at their breakfast bar, and she spun the now empty glass between her palms.

"I don't want to make anyone's life harder, Dylan. This story about Cameron's rescue is my first chance at a real article. I was excited about writing this epic piece that would secure my place at the Melbourne Herald. Now I'm not sure what the hell to write. But I assure you, I won't be outing you or your family in the press."

Things were getting way too serious and glum, so Dylan gave her his sly smirk. "How many dates do you normally go on before you 'fall into bed?'"

Ryan was standing behind Lacey and rolled his eyes at Dylan.

"You're an idiot, brother."

"Well, she was all sad and shit so I'm changing the subject."

"Um, I don't know! Six maybe?"

Dylan folded his arms over his chest as he leaned his butt against the kitchen counter opposite Lacey.

"Six dates, huh? Well, there are two of us, so that makes it three. It's Friday night now … and you've said you don't claim tonight as a date so Monday night you're all ours!"

He couldn't help but chuckle at the way Lacey's mouth opened and shut a few times. Her wide eyes looked so innocent as she struggled to deal with him. She finally closed her mouth and shook her head.

"You are too much, Dylan. Really? You think you can bargain your way into bed with me?"

"No. I'm negotiating dates with you, beautiful, and you'll be in both our beds, not just mine. Or rather, we'll both be in your bed. So, where do you live? We'll pick you up tomorrow at six for dinner."

Lacey laughed at him, the sadness leaving her face and the healthy bloom he'd admired when he'd first met her returning to her cheeks. "I have a work function tomorrow night. I guess I could meet up with you during the day."

The ache in Dylan's chest, which he hadn't even realized was there, eased a little with her words. She was agreeing to date them. They could do this. They could win her over and get her to agree to mate with them. He knew they could. Because they had to. If not, they'd be alone for the rest of their lives and be completely miserable.

CHAPTER SEVEN

He can't be for real. He just can't. Lacey blinked slowly. Once. Twice. She expected this fantasy of a man to vanish each time she reopened her eyes. He had to be a figment of her overactive imagine. Guess that's what I get for spending so much time with my head in a book.

After a third blink, she rubbed her eyes before glancing back at the hunk of a male standing in front of her. Nope, he was still there in all his glory. Damn, the man had to be six feet something and was mouth-wateringly yummy, even fully dressed. Wonder what his skin would taste like? She mentally shook her head. This was not the time for daydreams. This god of a man had just propositioned her. No, even more than that, he and his twin brother wanted to date her. She couldn't tell if it was a fantasy come true or a nightmare.

"Seriously, am I dreaming? Can someone pinch me or something?"

Dylan let out an inhuman growl. "I can show you an 'or something' that should clear things up for you."

He then strode towards her, erotic intent clear to read in his hot gaze.

With her stomach in knots, she squealed and jumped off her seat, bolting towards the door and where Ryan stood.

"No, no, stop! I was joking."

She held both hands out in front of her, her heart pounding in her chest. Dylan stopped in his tracks and tilted his head in an animalistic manner as Ryan shifted to stand between her and Dylan. Facing her, he cupped her cheek in his palm.

"Tell us what we can do to help you be okay with us."

His voice was so sweet, measured and calm. Such a contrast to the intense heat waves wafting off Dylan.

"There's nothing either of you can do. I need time to process everything I've learned today."

She bit her lip and looked between the brothers. Could she really do this? Date two men at once, and brothers at that? What would her friends think of her? Would she earn herself a reputation of being a slut? Would her friends leave her in the dust? Leaving her to start over.

"If I do this..."

"When you do this..." Dylan's deep, gravelly voice was so strong and confident, it sent liquid heat to pool between her thighs, which pissed her off. She was trying to be serious and think with her brain, not her lady parts. Damn, but he was far too sexy for her sanity on his own. What the hell would it be like when both of them were in full-on seduction mode?

"I want separate dates, to get to know you both better."

They looked stunned for a moment, their massive frames stilling in shock. Complete silence descended as they stared at each other. With a frown, she stamped her foot, which made them both turn towards her.

"Stop doing that! I hate it when you leave me out of the conversation."

Dylan chuckled, and Ryan gave her his lopsided smile.

"Sorry, beautiful. No one's ever picked up on it before. Our parents have always encouraged the connection so it's second nature to for us to use it."

She huffed in frustration as she put both her hands on her hips.

"I know it's a great thing for you two to have and I wouldn't normally care, except for the fact I know you're talking about me and that makes it unfair and rude."

Lacey coughed and cleared her throat, annoyed at how high-pitched her voice had become. She was probably being irrational, but at this point, she just didn't care.

Ryan reached out and stroked his palm over her forearm, the touch managing to both soothe her and make her ache for more.

"We were just tossing around ideas for our dates. If you want to see us separately to start with, we totally respect that."

"Yeah," Dylan interjected. "It'll be kinda nice to be treated like an individual person for once, rather than just half of one."

She snorted in a very inelegant way. "I hardly see you as half a person. You guys are too different to start with. You complement each other but are still very much separate. Everyone else must be cruel or plain stupid to not see that instantly."

She shook her head, suddenly furious at anyone who'd dared to treat these men badly in the past. She didn't know much about them yet, but the little she did know was enough to know they were decent men. They were brave, protectors of children, from a good family, had secure, steady jobs, and they were both clearly intelligent and capable of deep care and love. Listing it all off had Lacey back to thinking maybe she was still dreaming. These men were too perfect to exist in the real world.

They looked at each other again, and Lacey cleared her throat.

"Okay, so, you guys are happy for me to date you separately—"

Before she could finish, Ryan jumped in. "Yes. One date each, Saturday and Sunday, then Monday evening we'll go out together before we bring you back here. For the night."

She frowned, not sure she understood where this was going. If she decided to give these men a chance long-term, how the hell would it work? Did they expect her to allow them to take turns with her? A different twin every other night? That would be horrible. Her gut already twisted at the thought of a relationship that was so incredibly unorthodox.

But then again, would she be able to choose just one of them if her hand was forced? The good guy and the bad boy? Fire and ice. They were both so beautiful to her, and she felt a strong connection to each twin.

Her breath caught in her throat, and she frowned at the two men. Did they mean to share her in the sense that they'd both take her together? Like in the erotic fantasy novels she read. Warmth curled inside her, and she squeezed her eyes shut as she clenched her thigh muscles. No, no, no. That didn't happen in the real world! Maybe it would be best to just end this before it got going...

"And what happens if I can't date both of you, or it turns out we're not compatible?"

The men laughed, the sound so happy and husky that a shiver spread through her body and the heat between her legs coiled tighter until she ached. Why did she have such a visceral reaction to these men? Their smiles were so gorgeous she could barely hold onto her resolution to be strong. Her body and soul craved them and wanted her to quit fighting it and fall into their arms so she could bathe in their warmth and joy.

"What's so funny? My question was perfectly legitimate and a logical argument." Despite her resolve to remain serious, she felt her own lips turn up a little when the twins aimed their megawatt grins at her.

In a smooth, lightning-fast move, Dylan grabbed her around the waist and pulled her flush against his solid body. "Because, you, sweetheart, were made for us. You will fit with each of us like a lock and key, mind, body, and soul."

He slid his hands down to her ass and pulled her in snugly against his very erect flesh. She gasped as the ache between her legs increased tenfold.

"Not yet, buster." She pushed herself out of Dylan's arms but smiled at him to make sure he knew she wasn't trying to hurt his feelings.

"I really do need some time to myself to process all this. I'm going to head off." Underneath her worry and confusion, her heart felt light, an excitement flitting around her that she hadn't felt since she'd first received the offer for her university placement. "Which way is out?"

Ryan pushed open the kitchen door and pointed right. "We'll show you out. Just head through the lounge room and there's the front door."

Lacey walked into the entrance of the house and glanced around. "Wow, your house is beautiful." It had all the modern fittings but lacked a bit of warmth. There were a few photos around, but it was clearly an all-male household.

"Thanks. I'm glad you like it. We built it with you in mind."

She spun around and stared at them, her mirror image twins.

"Pardon me?" She couldn't have heard that right.

Dylan was shaking his head, and Ryan stepped forward, taking her hand and leading her towards the front door. "Sweetheart, you seem to have forgotten we are not human but cheetah shifters, born with only one mate. Because we're twins, Dylan and I, along with our parents, always assumed we would only have one wife between us. We built this house with you in mind. Waiting for the day when we finally found you."

Her brain took a little vacation as she stepped out the front door on autopilot. Taking a few deep breaths, inhaling the cool, clean air of their country property, she felt her body relax a little.

"So, are you saying you'd take turns with me or—you know..." She let the sentence drift, unsure how the hell to say what she was thinking.

Ryan stepped up to her and cupped her face with both his palms.

"However you need us to be, Lacey. We want everything with you. We both want to share your bed and your body every single night. But we can be patient and ease you into things, if that's what you need."

She cleared her throat while she tried to find the words to ask what she needed to know.

"So, have you guys ... you know?"

She swallowed hard as jealousy swam up inside her like ivy climbing a fence. Even with Ryan's calming touch, her emotions were swirling out of control. How many others had there been? How often? Was she just a notch in their bedpost and this whole mate thing was nothing but an elaborate pick-up line?

Dylan stepped up close to her, and Ryan dropped his hands to her shoulders. Dylan traced her cheekbone with a fingertip, the delicate touch sending ripples of heat through her body.

"Have we what?"

"You know... shared women before."

There was a moment of stunned silence and then an explosion of laughter around her, punctuated with comments like, "You're kidding, right?"

"Why would we do that?"

Both men had stepped away from her, and without Ryan's calming touch, rage overtook her mind. How dare they laugh at her! Again! Her cheeks burned furiously with a mix of embarrassment and anger. Clenching her jaw hard, she focused her attention on getting her bag. She marched over to her open window, reached into the car and dragged it out. She dug around in her things looking for her keys. She could hear them jingling. They must be in there.

"Hey, don't be mad at us, sweetheart. We're sorry, we weren't laughing at you."

"Yes, you were." She looked up and glared at them. She tucked her car keys into her back pocket, dropped her bag and then crossed her arms over her chest for emphasis.

"No, we really didn't mean to laugh at you. It's just that neither of us have ever dated anyone, let alone together. The very idea of having any kind of commitment to a woman who isn't our mate is simply unconceivable to us."

"You're kidding me." She dropped her arms as her seething temperature plummeted. Were they serious? These two men were beyond gorgeous, inside and out. They couldn't be virgins. Impossible! He had to mean something else.

Ryan shrugged. "Well, we've been told since we were young that we'd know when we found our mate by her scent, the instant attraction, and the perfection of her touch. It's called the Calling. We were waiting for you, and as soon as we saw you, we knew."

Lacey swallowed, salty tears swimming in her eyes, blurring her vision. She'd never been described as perfect by anyone—not even herself—and the idea that these two stunning men had been waiting for her made her want to cry.

"Okay, uh, so I'll see one of you tomorrow?"

She turned towards her car, her mind swimming in a cloud of disbelief. This was all so surreal. As she laid a hand on her door handle, her mind cleared a little, and she realized they hadn't made firm plans for tomorrow. Releasing her grip, she went to turn back toward the twins when Dylan's husky, deep voice rang out from just behind her.

"Hang on, beautiful. You're not leaving yet."

He took hold of her elbow, spinning her around before he pressed her up against the car with his body.

He stared down at her for a moment, and Lacey moaned as his lips descended, a blaze of heat engulfing her as his hands roamed up her body to cup her jaw moments before his lips connected with hers. With a contented sigh, she opened to him, and his tongue swept inside while he ground his hardening cock against her stomach.

She groaned and let her knees give way when he pressed into her deeper, holding her weight easily as she grabbed fistfuls of his shirt, yanking it upwards so she could slide her hands beneath the cotton to feel his hot flesh. His skin was smooth and perfect, just like the rest of him.

He tore his mouth away and stared down at her with a gaze so full of lust, she was surprised she didn't go up in flames.

"Come back inside, beautiful." His voice was barely discernable through his low growl, but she knew what he was asking her.

"I can't."

He stared at her a moment longer before he sighed and closed his eyes as he rested his forehead against hers.

Gosh, but she was a fool. Could she resist them until Monday night? She was one hundred percent sure she couldn't say no to either of them if they pushed her even a little right now.

Lacey stood up a little straighter and rested against him, unable to believe that an attraction like this truly existed for her. She'd never wanted anyone this much in her entire life.

She kept her hands where they were beneath his shirt and stroked the skin over his tight abs in a gentle caress, craving the connection with him while she ached to be closer.

Dylan purred in his throat as his body quivered beneath her touch. Eventually, he heaved a tormented sounding sigh and pushed away from her.

She wanted to cry out as the cold air rushed into the place his warm body had been, but she knew that would lead to her going back inside their house. So, she resolutely stayed put, clinging to the car to prevent herself from falling to the ground.

Ryan stayed silent but watched intently as his twin stiffly walked back to stand beside him. "Can you meet me at the zoo tomorrow? We're both working, but I thought I could give you a tour of the grounds and maybe have some lunch. Say, ten at the main gate?"

Lacey nodded and tried to smile but failed, her lips feeling swollen and sore. In a completely delicious way.

"That sounds perfect, Ryan. Thanks."

Before she forgot her mind and threw herself at them, Lacey slipped into her car, forcing her mushy legs to move as she studiously ignored her pussy, which was now wet and aching for the twins, who had proved how easily they could arouse her.

"I'll see you tomorrow," she called out through her open window as she waved at Ryan and Dylan, who were smiling at her from where they stood near their front door. An ache bloomed in her chest as she turned the car around and drove off the property, but she refused to give in and return to them.

"Oh. My. Gosh." She glanced in her rearview mirror almost constantly while navigating the long dirt driveway off the farm. She had two dates for the weekend and a set of twins who were hell bent on winning her over.

She took a shuddering breath then giggled with nerves as she cranked up the radio. She had a feeling that no matter what happened with the twins, her life would never be the same again. She couldn't wait.

CHAPTER EIGHT

Ryan frowned as he tracked the dust cloud that followed his mate's car as she drove further from them. His gut was churning, and his erection was straining against the front of his jeans, not at all happy about missing out on claiming the sweetly sexy Lacey.

Dylan growled low from where he stood beside him, obviously feeling the same way. He turned to face his twin before he spoke. "Nice move with halving the six dates to three, by the way."

"Yeah, well, I wasn't letting her get away with putting us off for a bloody month! I'm pretty sure if we'd let her, she'd have only let us have one date a week in an attempt to spread this thing out."

Ryan grimaced. His twin had a point. Lacey was going to make them work for her, and in a way, he respected her all the more for it. No way did he want a passive mate who just agreed with everything he or Dylan suggested. That would quickly get boring, and after growing up with a mother like theirs, a weak female wouldn't be respected by any of their family. A hard slap to his shoulder snapped him out of his introspection.

"Let's go grab a beer. I need a drink."

"I think I need a very cold shower first. Damn, but my entire body is just about vibrating with need for her."

Dylan grunted as he pushed his way through their front door and into their house.

"Just think how you'll feel by morning, Ry. With Lacey having slept on your bed, it's all you're going to be able to smell. All. Night. Long."

"It'll be a bitch, but at least I'll have sweet dreams. Admit it, you're so fucking jealous of me right now."

Ryan knew his brother was envious. He could see it in the tense set of his jaw and shoulders. Technically Ryan's bed was big enough for him and his brother, but without Lacey between them, he had zero intention of sharing with his twin.

"How'd you end up with the master bedroom when I'm the eldest?"

Ryan turned to his twin with a wide grin. "Because I won the coin toss, remember? Mum got sick of us bickering and made us agree to stick with whoever won."

Dylan buried his head in the fridge with a grunt instead of answering. A moment later, he handed Ryan an ice-cold beer. Ryan snatched the fancy magnet that doubled as a bottle opener off the fridge door and popped open his brew to take a deep drink.

"Oh, yeah. That's what I needed." He paused to take another swig, the cold hops soothing his heated core. This worked so much quicker than a cold shower and was more enjoyable, too.

"C'mon, let's go have a game."

Dylan grinned as he nodded. "Sounds perfect."

Ryan followed his brother to the other end of their house to the large game room. Their centerpiece was a beautifully handcrafted pool table. No standard green top for them, their felt was a rich, bright red and the pockets made from dark leather. The timber of the table was stained black, and all together it created one hell of a stunning piece of furniture. It had been their housewarming gift from their brothers. Of course, most of their brothers were around here on a Saturday night playing on it with them.

Ryan got two cues ready as Dylan went to the table to rack up the balls.

"You wanna break?"

"Nah, you can do it."

Dylan sauntered up to Ryan and switched the white ball for a cue. Both he and Dylan had always liked playing pool. There was something almost hypnotic about it that instantly had them both hooked from their first game.

Carefully placing the white ball inside the D on the felt, Ryan lowered his body over the table to take first shot. Two smalls went into pockets, and Ryan grinned. Perfect break. He rolled his right shoulder as he moved around the table and planned his next shot.

"You are not going to pot out on me, Ry. Not on our first fucking game."

"So what if I do? It's not like we're down the pub and paying two bucks a game."

"Hardly a game if I don't get a shot. Just tone it down. We're home, not playing the state titles or anything."

Yeah, okay, so maybe Dylan had a point. But Ryan couldn't help it. He got his head in the game and that was that. He bent forward and lined up his next shot.

He grimaced when one of Dylan's balls followed his into the pocket. There went any hope of potting out.

"Damn. Two shots to you."

Ryan moved to grab his drink. With two shots, it was Dylan who would pot out on him and finish the game in no time. Dylan potted three balls in short order then stopped to re-chalk his cue.

"Hey, Dylan, don't suppose you nabbed Lacey's phone number while you were messing with her phone earlier?"

Dylan stopped still and glared over at him. "Seriously? I wasn't fucking messing with her phone, Ry."

Ryan rolled his eyes. Damn, but Dylan could be a drama queen.

"I don't care what you call what you did with her phone. I just want to know if you got her number."

His glower evaporated and a smirk replaced it.

"Of course, I did. If you'd check your phone once in a while, you'd have seen the text already."

With a frown, Ryan slid his phone from his pocket to check it.

"Damn, it's still on silent."

He swiped the screen to open up the message and saw the sweetest ten digits with a message below stating, "Lacey phone".

"Thanks, Dylan. What do you say we shoot her a message each?"

"Yeah, sounds like a plan. We forgot to find out where she lives. I'd like to know she got home safely."

"I'll ask her tomorrow."

As Dylan pulled his own phone from his pocket, and Ryan started tapping out his message, excitement coursed through Ryan's system. He'd get all day with his mate tomorrow, and he couldn't fucking wait.

"Wow." Lacey twirled on her toes and let herself go, falling backwards onto her bed, the soft mattress cushioning her weight as she bounced a little.

She had never been so excited yet so confused at the same time. First was the fact that she'd discovered a family of cheetah shifters.

Oh. My. Gosh!

"You can say that again."

With a grin, she rolled onto her side, curling up into a fetal position as she tucked a pillow beneath her head.

Were there more of them? Or were Ryan and Dylan's family the only ones? That seemed unlikely, so she had to assume there were more, probably a lot more. Were there only cheetah shifters or other breeds, too?

Her thoughts took a more personal twist. Would their children be shifters? Or normal like her? When they mated her, would she become like them? Or remain human?

She groaned and rolled her eyes at herself.

"Stop it, stop it, stop it! You're getting way ahead of yourself, Lacey-girl."

She slapped a hand to her forehead and laughed. It was all so ridiculous, it was hard not to let her imagination run wild. Who would have thought a family with nine sons would exist? Even if they were fully human, they'd be an anomaly. Add in that two of those sons were a set of identical mirror image twins who thought she was their destined soul mate … just wow. It was all too much for her mind to process.

Her phone buzzed, and she crawled to the edge of the bed to grab it from where she'd tossed it on her nightstand.

"Oh, for fuck's sake…"

She groaned again as she opened message, seeing the last abusive message her ex had sent her, the one Dylan had seen, then his new one.

You're home. Good. Come let me in.

She shivered as the hairs prickled on her arms and a shot of adrenaline had her racing to the front door.

She checked the dead bolt. Yep, it was tight.

She moved from room to room, turning lights on as she went, clutching her mobile in her hand in case she needed to make a phone call quickly.

The house was small, and as soon as she had every light in the place on and was certain both doors and all windows were locked tight, she messaged her roommate, checking when she'd be home.

When she walked past hall closet, she saw the cricket bat leaning up against it and snatched it up as added protection on her way back to her bedroom. Placing the bat within easy reach, she settled on the mattress once more, feeling a little safer after having checked everything was locked up and the house was empty. She took a couple of slow breaths, trying to will her heart rate to slow down even a little. It wasn't healthy to be so scared of someone.

Lacey sat in the center of her bed, all lights on, cricket bat by her side and her mobile in her hand. Maybe it was time to try blocking him again, although the last time she'd done that, he'd came back on a new number within hours making all sorts of threats the cops couldn't do anything about because he'd not actually done anything to her. Yet.

Even though she'd given up trying to block him, she generally didn't reply to any of his messages—she had been told not to engage with him at all, but as the butterflies in her stomach finally calmed down, the heat and tightness of anger set in. How dare he continue to do this to her?

She lifted her phone into her line of sight and stared at the screen for a moment, then started to type.

No. I don't want to see you. We broke up three months ago. Please stop contacting me.

She sent it, and within thirty seconds another message popped up.

You can't just throw me away like that. We're meant to be together. I love you.

"Argh!" Lacey threw her phone onto her pillows and went to the bathroom to get ready for bed. She squeezed toothpaste onto her brush before she shook her head as she glared in the mirror at her reflection.

Who the hell did he think he was? And why they hell had she gone out with him in the first place? She scrubbed her teeth hard as the memories flooded in. Rodney had been nice at the start. Complimented her quite a bit, wanted to be with her all the time. It'd been nice, kind of. After so many years of being single it had been good to be in a couple, to see how the other half lived. But Rodney had soon become possessive and controlling, and once those traits came out, she'd gotten away from him as quickly as she could.

"Hey, Lacey! I'm home."

Laura's voice made her jump and she screamed out, only to have her best friend bolt to the bathroom and throw the door open.

"You okay?"

Lacey put her toothbrush down and took a deep breath as she gripped the sides of the sink. Her heart was pounding so hard she felt like she was going to vomit.

"Yeah, you just startled me."

Laura's mouth turned down, her eyes widening. "That wanker contact you again? Is that why every single light in this place is on?"

Lacey nodded, shrugging as she gripped her toothbrush again.

"You know, we could move."

Lacey winced at Laura's suggestion. She'd already moved once since she'd broken up with Rodney.

"He'd just find me again. Just like he always finds my phone number."

"Well, just remember, if you want to move to escape the bastard, just say the word and we're off to somewhere new."

Not wanting to talk about her stupid ex anymore, Lacey decided to try distraction.

"Hey, Laura, can I ask you a question?"

Laura leaned against the door, her gorgeous, long blonde hair falling over her perfect little boobs. "Yeah, 'course."

Lacey frowned as she thought about how to frame the question. What was the real root of her problem?

"Shit, I don't know how to phrase it."

"Well, what's the problem?"

"I met these guys. Twins, actually."

Laura's face lit up with a huge smile. "Yeah, and?"

"They're part of a story I'm writing, and they invited me back to their place for dinner to work on it, but when I got there, their whole family was there to meet me."

"Oh wow, that's a bit fast, isn't it?"

Lacey pushed out a laugh at the concerned look on her friend's face.

You don't know the half of it.

"I suppose. What I want to know is, what would you do if you fell for a guy..." Or guys, "who was different, or that wanted an unconventional relationship that other people wouldn't understand or approve of?"

Laura pushed herself up from the doorframe and cocked her head. "Lace, the only thing I know about relationships is that they're hard work. If you can find someone you love, who returns that love and who treats you how you deserve to be treated, what does it matter what the world thinks? The world doesn't have to live in your back pocket. You know that my parents have a bit of a weird marriage, right?"

Lacey nodded as Laura glanced away for a moment. Her parents' open relationship was a difficult topic for her to talk about at any time.

"Yeah, well, it works for them. There's one hundred percent honesty between them. They've worked out what they both need and then found a way to keep each other happy. I know I couldn't do it, but, hey, who am I to judge? If I could actually find a halfway decent guy, who knows what I'd do to keep him?"

Lacey smiled at her best friend, a gorgeous woman who'd had more than her fair share of cheating, nasty, lazy boyfriends.

"You're right, Laura, thanks. I suppose I hadn't thought about it like that."

Laura gave her a wink and headed off to her room, turning off lights as she went, leaving Lacey alone to contemplate her friend's words.

You'll never know how you'll cope in any situation until you're actually in it.

Well, she was faced with a door into an unknown world, and it was her choice whether she leapt forward or stayed right where she was.

She headed back to her room and heard her phone buzz again.

She picked it up and blinked at the screen. Fours new messages. Wow.

One was from her ex.

We're meant to be together Lacey. I'll do anything. Just tell me what you need, baby.

"Oh, great. Mr. Hyde is out to play tonight."

Her ex had two very distinct sides. One was very nice, the other nasty as could be. She tried not to listen to the charming sweetheart, because the asshole side would be back within a matter of minutes most days. She refused to let fear and her idiotic ex rule her life, but you had to be clever sometimes, too.

The second message was from her mother.

Your father told me that you have your first proper assignment. Please email it to me on Sunday morning so I have time to check it before you submit it.

Lacey shuddered on a groan. Her mother hadn't taken a lot of interest in her while she was growing up, but now that she was an adult and had a decent job, one that would potentially land her in the limelight of a large newspaper, all of a sudden, she wanted to be friends?

"I don't think so."

The last two messages were from numbers she didn't have, and as she opened them a smile broke out across her lips.

Hey, Lacey, good night, beautiful. Can't wait until Sunday! Dylan

She grinned and opened the second one.

Hey, Lacey, hope you don't mind that Dylan grabbed your number from your phone earlier. We just wanted to check you got home all right. Hope you sleep well. See you tomorrow. Love, Ryan.

She scrolled up and saw that Dylan had sent a message to both himself and Ryan from her phone earlier in the evening. He must have done it after seeing that message from her ex. She quickly tapped out a reply to them both letting them know she was home safe and would see Ryan tomorrow.

Soaring high from her men's sweet messages of care and concern, she quickly changed into her pajamas and floated into bed where she snuggled down under the comforter. Which she realized wasn't as soft as Ryan's had been.

Was there really any choice for her to make? Would leaving her past of pain, mental abuse and not being appreciated behind to explore what could be with two men who believed she was perfect for them in every way really be so bad?

She rolled onto her side and let her eyes slowly shut against the soft glow in her room. She'd turned off all the lights except her nightlight. As she did every night, she left that one on just be certain no one was in her room with her if she woke during the night.

"I guess that means I've made my decision, then."

It really was a no-brainer.

CHAPTER NINE

Snatching his radio from his belt, Ryan checked it was working for probably the tenth time in the last half hour. Lacey was late. He moved his thumb to press the button to speak with the gatehouse but stopped before the connection was made. Shelley hadn't been impressed with his constant hassling, or that's what she'd called it after the fourth time he'd talked to her. One more call and she'd probably refuse to let Lacey in.

"Why don't you get some work done, son? It'll help the time pass. I'm sure she's simply been held up with traffic."

He hoped his dad was right and they hadn't lost their mate before they'd even begun. Ryan cracked his neck and rolled his shoulders attempting to release some of the tension in his body. Every muscle was tight and aching.

"The next tasks I have are all time-consuming ones out in the exhibits, and ones I was hoping to take Lacey with me."

If he left and missed her, she'd be waiting an hour for him to come back. What sort of first date would that be?

"I understand, but you're up to help with the public feeding of the giraffes. They can't be left waiting for their food for too long. Visitors will be crowding the viewing platform waiting for you. You have ten minutes, and then you'll have no choice but to go. I'll take Lacey to Dylan until you get back if she comes while you're out there."

After having an enforced week off due to their punishment for saving Cameron, Ryan had extra jobs outside his normal ones with the cheetahs and lions. Normally, he didn't mind helping out with the other areas of the zoo, but today Ryan's usual calm had deserted him, and he nearly snarled at his father. Damn giraffes could wait all bloody day for all he cared. Stupid beasts could always go pick their own damn leaves. Lazy bastards.

"Stop frowning, Ryan. You can take her this afternoon. It's Saturday, which means they get fed twice today. I would have thought you'd be more interested in showing her around the cheetah exhibit, anyway. Go take her to say hi to Max. I'm sure he could use a friendly face."

Ryan winced. He'd momentarily forgotten about his brother's punishment. Poor cat had ten long days ahead of him stuck in the feeding yard being gawked at by tourists and hand fed raw meat. He shuddered. Raw meat was only worth eating if you could go catch it yourself. Otherwise, you may as well be in human form so you could cook it up and make it taste decent.

"Yeah, I might sneak in a treat for him."

Maybe he could get Dylan to bake a whole fish for Max.

"I need to see Dylan before Lacey gets here. I'll talk to you later, Dad."

He all but sprinted out of his father's office and over to the restaurant. He slipped into the kitchen and found his twin alone in the large room chopping up vegetables with way too much enthusiasm.

"Hey, bro."

Dylan paused mid slice to glance over at him. The grin that had lit up Dylan's face faded fast, and it made Ryan feel like a heel. No doubt, Dylan was hoping he'd snuck in with Lacey.

"Sorry, Dylan. She's not here yet. I was just wondering if you could do me a favor?"

"If I can. What's up?"

"Max has already started doing his time in the feeding yard, and I was wondering if you had a trout or something in the fridge that you could bake whole for him? I'll let Lacey give it to him."

With a chuckle and a shake of his head, Dylan put down his knife and turned to face Ryan with his arms crossed over his chest.

"You feeling guilty over him being punished, Ry?"

"Maybe a little. Max might have started it, but what happened in the end? We were all at fault, and Lacey wasn't hurt, just shocked. Besides, ten days stuck in one form is going to hurt like a bitch."

Even Dylan grimaced at that point.

"Knowing Dad, Max won't serve more than seven and you know it."

Ryan had already considered that would be the case. Especially considering how bloody smooth their brother could be when he wanted to be. He'd managed to charm his way out of nearly every punishment their mother set for him during his teenage years. Ryan wasn't sure how he did it, but he was a genius at getting around their parents... most of the time.

"So, do you have something lying around you can spare for him?"

"Yeah, I'll find something. What time will you be heading over there?"

"I've got to deal with the giraffes first. Then I was planning on taking Lacey up to the cheetahs. That's if she ever turns up."

His ten minutes were just about up, and he was about to tell Dylan he'd get to spend the morning with her when his radio crackled, and Shelley paged him to the front gatehouse.

"'Bout fucking time."

He agreed with his twin's statement as relief coursed through Ryan and he sighed aloud. He wouldn't have to leave her behind for his morning jobs, and that knowledge made all the tension in his muscles leech out and left him feeling relaxed.

"Okay, I'll catch you later. Maybe we'll head over to Max after lunch. That'll give you enough time?"

"Sure thing, Ry. Let me know when you come in to eat. I'll prepare her something special."

With a chuckle, Ryan bolted from the kitchen and out to the parking lot. With his heart thumping hard against his ribs from both joy and excitement, he jumped in one of the park's buggies to go collect his mate. Today was going to be a very good day.

Shit, shit, shit!

"Did you call him?"

As she waited for the woman behind the counter to respond, Lacey twisted her fingers together while she practically hopped on the spot. She couldn't believe she was so late!

"Yes, he's on his way so would you relax, please? You're as bad as he is, calling me every two minutes..." The woman gave her a solid glare then shooed her away. "Go stand over there."

"Thank you!" Lacey grabbed her bag and danced over to the stand in front of a large sign that showed a map of the entire zoo. Damn, this place was huge. When she caught sight of the cheetah exhibit's location, her blood heated, and her palms grew sweaty. Her heart was still pounding hard after the morning she'd had. Now the anticipation of seeing Ryan was adding to it, she was beginning to feel a little faint.

"Lacey!"

She turned at the sound of Ryan's voice to see him jogging over to her, his beautiful smile in place. A feeling of inadequacy washed over her in a hot wave. How could this perfect man want her? She was little Miss Average, and she couldn't even manage to turn up for their date on time!

"Ryan, I am so, so sorry I'm late! I had a flat tire, then I had to wait for roadside assistance to arrive, and you don't answer your phone so I couldn't tell you! And..."

Ryan grabbed a hold of her waist, pulled her against his warm body and planted a fast, hard kiss on her lips before he pulled back with a grin.

Lacey blinked up at him, that strange tightness in her belly disappearing now that she knew he wasn't upset with her.

"No problem, I'm just happy you made it. Come on, we have to hurry. I'm late."

Guilt had her wincing as he took her hand and pulled her through a side door that was labeled "Staff Only." She had to jog to keep up with his fast pace as they made their way over to a small ute with a flatbed on the back loaded up with branches.

"Ryan Monaghan, report in your location." The walkie-talkie buzzed for a moment after the man's deep—angry sounding—voice faded.

With a curse, Ryan put the device close to his mouth,

"Yeah, I'm in the buggy and on my way now."

Ryan motioned to the vehicle and grinned at her. "Jump in."

Lacy nodded and did as he said while Ryan turned the engine on, threw it into gear, and they took off.

"Whoa." Lacey scrabbled for her seatbelt as Ryan chuckled. He had his on, but she couldn't recall seeing him fasten it. When did he have time to do that?

"I'm so sorry about being late. I hope I haven't gotten you into trouble."

Ryan glanced at her and grinned, then looked back at the track he was driving along. A moment later they stopped in front of a tall wire gate. He pushed a button on a remote that was stuck to the dash and with a rattle and a squeak, the gate rolled to the side, allowing them entrance into the open paddock on the other side.

"No worries. I'm sorry I couldn't get to my phone, but we can't have them on us at work. Did you say you had a flat tire?"

Lacey nodded, chewing on her bottom lip. "Yeah, although it had some help." She paused a moment. How much should she tell him? He and Dylan had seemed so careful with her last night. Surely, they wouldn't condone her ex's actions or hold her to blame for them. "It was, um, sort of slashed. I think my ex might be up to his old tricks again."

Ryan glanced at her once more, this time with thunder in his gaze and a deep frown marring his beautiful face.

"How often does he do shit like this?"

Lacey shrugged and wanting a distraction, looked ahead. She gasped at the beauty of what she saw. A small herd of giraffes had gathered near a raised viewing platform, which was rather high off the ground. There were heaps of people up there, all taking photos and making lots of excited noises.

"Wow. What are we doing?"

Ryan smiled as the animals moved to allow him to pull up next to a tall pole with chains hanging from it that she'd not noticed earlier. He turned off the engine and unbuckled his seatbelt before he answered her.

"We're feeding giraffes."

He jumped out of the vehicle and hopped up on the tray where he pulled the chain over and began attaching branches to it. With all the little round yellow flowers, it had to be wattle that he was hooking up for them.

Lacey curled up sideways on the seat so she could watch him work. The way his muscled arms flexed beneath his short-sleeved shirt was simply captivating.

Lacey yelped as a few of the massive yellow and brown animals that hadn't already been waiting for them began loping towards her from across the paddock. Gosh, they were huge up close!

"Holy moly." Keeping her gaze on the giraffes that were rapidly approaching, she subconsciously began pushing back against the door as she strained her neck to watch through the rear window as the giraffe began nibbling on the branches Ryan had sent up the pole. She'd not seen how Ryan got the branches up so high but figured the chains must be on a pulley or something.

He smoothly moved from the tray and got back into the driver's seat. Starting the vehicle, he drove over closer to the raised platform before stopping once more.

"Come on, Lacey, hop out and join me."

Lacey scrambled to undo her seat belt and slid out of the vehicle. Ryan was there to help her. Wrapping his strong warm hands around her waist, he lifted her easily up onto the tray. He quickly followed her up, and a shudder of pleasure ran through her as Ryan wrapped his arm around her shoulders and gave her a squeeze.

"Don't be scared, beautiful girl. These animals are gentle. Just lean against me and enjoy it. Being this close is pretty damn surreal, isn't it?"

Lacey nodded as her heart raced in her chest as excitement, fear, and arousal warred inside her. She knew that they wouldn't attack her, but it was intimidating, to say the least.

"They're just so huge."

The animals kept on chewing, and Ryan pressed his lips to the top of her head, inhaling against her hair.

"You smell so good."

"Ryan..." Lacey admonished as she wiggled against him. Her nipples tightened, and heat warmed her cheeks. She was far too aware of how devastatingly handsome this man was.

"Sorry ... damn. Uh, did you know that giraffes have seven vertebrae in their neck just like we do?"

"Really? That's incredible, especially considering the length of theirs compared to ours."

Lacey stared up at the animals that couldn't possibly share a similar anatomical characteristic with her. There was just too much of a difference.

"Yeah, really. They get a second feeding this afternoon. If you want, you can go up on the boardwalk and hear the talk."

Lacey glanced up to see a uniformed woman animatedly chatting away to the crowd of tourists, obviously about the giraffes.

She glanced back at the pole just as a smaller giraffe left the branches and came toward them.

"Um, Ryan? What's that one doing?"

Ryan chuckled as he released her shoulders and dug his hand into his pants' pocket.

"This cheeky girl is after a carrot. Want to feed it to her?"

Images of losing a finger clouded her mind. "Uh, no. That's okay. I'll just watch you do it."

He gave her a smirk with a raised eyebrow, like he knew she was being a coward, but fortunately he didn't comment. He moved to the back of the tray and held the carrot out for the young giraffe. The animal took it gently with its long tongue and quickly ate it. Naturally, the animal came back in for another until Ryan held his hands out. "All gone, sweet girl."

Totally spellbound, Lacey stared as the animal lumbered back to the few remaining branches still tangled in the chains. "We better head back for lunch and then I'll take you up to the cheetah area."

Lacey grinned and got back into the vehicle, buckling up and tapping her hands on her thighs with excitement.

"Awesome."

Ryan chuckled again as they began driving back. "So, this isn't too boring of a first date?"

Lacey laughed, unable to keep the noise inside. "This is the best date ever. I can't believe you get to do this every day."

She smiled as they bounced their way over the track and back through the gate. She felt so happy whenever she was around either of these two men, and Ryan had such a good aura. It settled her instantly and made her feel like she'd finally found her home.

They pulled up in front of a large, glass-fronted building, and Ryan turned off the ute.

"Let's go see Dylan at the restaurant. He said he was making you something special."

"Oh, I can't wait!"

Her chest tightened at the idea that she would soon see Dylan, the dark and sexy one. That man brought out every little part of her that had always been attracted to the bad boys. He exuded an air of Alpha male all the time.

Ryan took her hand as they walked along the path through a beautifully designed native garden, his easy confidence making her sigh. People turned their heads and watched them as they moved past, and Lacey felt a smile lift her lips. Ryan looked so healthy and strong in his uniform, and she was proud to be standing beside him.

"After you." He opened the door and indicated the way with a flourish of his hand and a smile.

"Well, thank you, kind sir."

She winked at him as she stepped through, her breath catching in her throat as Dylan's impressive figure walked towards her, a grin plastered all over his gorgeous face.

"Hey, beautiful."

Dylan stopped before her and held up his hands. He made quite the statement in his white chef uniform. The paleness of the clothing seemed to make his shoulders look broader, and it also made him look taller. "Can't kiss you out here in the open while I'm on the clock unfortunately, because you have no idea how much I want to do just that. You here to eat?"

With her mouth suddenly dry, she couldn't speak so settled for nodding. Heat bloomed between her thighs as her eyes roamed over his face. The spiky black hair, the liquid chocolate eyes, and the strong square jaw...

Yum.

"Good, grab a seat and I'll send your meal out shortly."

He nodded at his twin, and Ryan put a hand around her waist, directing her towards a square table set against the back wall and in a corner. Nice and private, for an open plan style restaurant. The whole place was so clean for being inside a zoo, she was impressed already. There was a great buzzing atmosphere, too, with all the families settled in at the tables around the glass walls.

"Is your brother a good cook?"

Ryan barked out a laugh as they slid onto their seats, his eyes bright and mischievous.

"I try my best not to blow up his self image any more than it currently is, but yeah, he's damn talented."

A waitress walked up with two plates and set them down in front of them.

"Enjoy." She smiled and stared at Lacey for a second longer than she should have, then walked away.

"What was that about?" Lacey asked, indicating to the waitress as she walked away.

Ryan shrugged. "Probably just curious. I've heard rumors about me being gay because I don't fall into bed with every female who offers." He picked up his knife and fork and inhaled deeply. "Oh, this smells good."

Lacey glanced down and smiled at the beautiful plate of food. So many colors.

"Looks great."

She picked up her own fork and took a bite of the rice and curry concoction. "Hmmm." She nodded and chewed, flavors exploding across her tastebuds. Coconut rice, chicken satay and vegetables, all balanced with perfect creaminess and freshness.

"So, you haven't had many girlfriends then?"

She took a sip of water and waited as Ryan finished his mouthful.

"No, not at all. Like we explained last night, I knew that Dylan and I would probably share a mate and that we'd know her when we met her. There was no point bonding with someone else and then hurting her when I found you."

Lacey grinned and hid it while eating her food. "But you have had..."

Heat flushed her cheeks, and she swallowed. She couldn't say it.

"What? Sex? Well, yeah. Just nothing long-term."

Lacey's stomach dropped as hot envy pulsed through her. It was unreasonable, of course. She'd had men in her bed before meeting them too, but she hated to think of Ryan or Dylan with anyone but her.

He must have seen her inner turmoil because he reached over and squeezed her hand.

"I had to make sure I knew what to do to pleasure my mate once I found her. No way was I going to risk losing her because I couldn't fulfill all of her needs."

Shock had Lacey choking on her mouthful of rice, and she grabbed for her glass of water. All of her sexual experiences with her ex-lovers had been uncomfortable, over way too quickly, and had left her always feeling extremely unfulfilled. There had never been any orgasms, not on her side of the fence anyway, and certainly none of the soul-bonding passion that she'd always been hoping for.

"You, ah, pardon?"

Ryan grinned at her. "I can't speak for Dylan, but I've made it my mission to become the best lover possible. I'm only twenty-three, of course, so I haven't become an expert or anything. But now that I've found you, I intend to learn everything you need and desire, then give it all to you and more. And, Lacey? I can't wait to start."

CHAPTER TEN

With his heart pounding, Dylan rushed through the last of the lunch orders so he could get out to Lacey. His hands were literally shaking as he flipped burgers and arranged salads. Despite her insistence that he and Ryan take turns to date her, he was going to crash their date. To hell with waiting, he had to see her.

He glanced over the head-high counter and noted the short line. So long as he could get all these orders done and out before they finished their meal, he'd be there to see her enjoy the special, completely off menu dessert he'd made for her.

He glanced up at the clock, clenching his teeth together as he quickly calculated the time. They'd had twenty minutes to eat already, and he was sure Ryan had other things planned for the afternoon.

Damn, he hoped they hadn't left already. He slapped the bell, sliding the last plate onto the heating tray and made a dash for the fridge. He opened the glass doors and grabbed the plated desserts he'd come in especially early to prepare for his mate. Snatching up a couple of forks and spoons on his way through the door, he headed to the back corner where Ryan had sat with Lacey. His breath left his lungs in a rush when he saw that they were still there. The table was clear of dishes, and Lacey looked like she was reaching for her bag.

"You don't have to leave just yet, do you, Ryan?"

His twin glanced at his watch.

"Nah, we still have some time."

He placed the plates onto the table and sat down next to Lacey, making sure he moved close enough to feel the warmth of her thigh against his own. She had Ryan on one side and him on the other. How it should be.

"Hope you like strawberries, beautiful."

He carefully moved one plate in front of Lacey before he handed the other to Ryan.

"This looks amazing, Dylan. The bowls are so gorgeous. How did you do it? Or do you buy them like that?"

"I made it all from scratch. Well, except for the fresh strawberries, obviously." He paused to wink at her. "The chocolate bowls are made by dipping a balloon in melted chocolate. Then they're filled with a vanilla bean whipped cream and topped with plenty of the finest berries I could find."

Pride swelled in his chest as his mate stared at him in awe, her big, hazel eyes shiny and wide.

"You made that sound so simple when I'm certain it's not. I can't wait to try it." She reached over and tangled her fingers with his. "Thank you, Dylan. I can't believe you went to all this effort just for me."

A lump rose in his throat, making it impossible for him to speak. He loved to cook, and the fact that she obviously appreciated the effort he'd put in to make this simple dessert for her brightened his day. Moving his hand so he had hers palm up, he raised them until he could press a kiss against the soft, sensitive skin of her palm, a sly grin forming as he heard her gasp in a breath.

"Eat up, Lacey. I believe Ryan's not finished with the activities he has planned for you today."

With a slight shake of her head, she pulled her hand from his and set about delicately eating her dessert.

"So, Dylan, how'd you do with what I requested this morning? Any luck?"

Without taking his gaze from Lacey who was moaning as she swallowed the first mouthful, he responded to his twin.

"Yeah, there's a baked trout in the warmer ready to go."

With a quirked eyebrow, Lacey glanced toward him, and when she saw him staring at her, a sweet blush colored her cheeks.

"What on earth are you two planning to do with a whole baked fish?"

Ryan ran his fingers down her cheek before cradling her jaw and turning her to face him.

"You remember last night at my parents' place? How things got out of hand? Dad gave Max a punishment for starting it."

His sweet mate dropped her spoon, and it made a clanging noise as it collided with the plate. She gasped, her mouth opening into a large O. "Oh, no! It's not his fault I freaked out."

Ryan's thumb moved to stroke the line of her jaw, and Dylan couldn't look away.

Fuck, that's hot.

"We could have and should have handled telling you about us so much better. But I agree, it wasn't all his fault, but he's copping the punishment for it. He has to spend ten days here in the feeding yard in his cheetah form."

"Feeding yard?"

"There're two areas for the cheetahs. One is a large, open plain area where the tour buses drive through. The other is a smaller area with a raised caged platform where people can get quite close to the cheetahs. There are never more than three animals in there. Twice a day they get publicly fed. Great big chunks of raw meat. Max isn't going to be very happy in there for all the world to gawk at him."

Lacey covered Ryan's fingers with her own before she lowered his hand from her face. With a frown of concentration marring her beautiful face, she ate another small bite of her dessert.

"But he's in animal form, right? So, he thinks like an animal, not a human?"

Ryan had just filled his mouth with a large piece of his own creamy dessert, so Dylan took up explaining.

"Our animal half isn't a separate entity. We're one being. We have the same thought patterns whether we're in human or cheetah form. For example, Ryan and I would do anything to keep you safe as men. If we were in cheetah form and someone threatened you? We wouldn't think twice about defending you. We would know exactly who you are to us, no matter what form we are in. Keeping you safe is our number one priority, especially as you're our mate."

Lacey coughed. "We've only just met. You can't possibly feel so much for me already."

Dylan shrugged, a grin spreading across his face. "You were always meant to be ours, Lacey. But if you need some time to see it's real, that's fine. Ryan and I will just keep proving it to you."

Slowly chewing another mouthful, Dylan could see her plotting questions.

"So why is Max going to be unhappy? Other than being watched while he eats."

His mate was an inquisitive little thing, and good at avoiding topics she didn't want to talk about. Duh, of course she is. She's a reporter.

"We need to spend time in each form. We can't remain in either our human or animal state for long periods of time without becoming uncomfortable in our skin. The aches turn to pain, which becomes debilitating agony if we stay in one form for a really long time. Ten days is pushing close to that limit. That, and the other reason Max will be grumpy is that he's being fed nothing but raw meat. Even as a cheetah, we're human enough to like our food cooked and seasoned."

She smirked up at him. "Are you trying to tell me if you were in cheetah form and a rabbit ran in front of you, you wouldn't hunt it down for a snack?"

"That's different, beautiful. Stalking and hunting our own prey is great fun and the only time we don't mind eating raw meat. And in that case, it would still be warm, so nothing like the cold lumps of lamb or beef they'll be tossing at Max for the next ten days."

Lacey screwed up her face. "Eww, Dylan, that's just gross."

Dylan shrugged with a chuckle.

"I am what I am."

Lacey took the final bite of her dessert and sighed, her shoulders sagging while a happy smile lifted her beautiful lips. Ryan took her now free hand in his and got her attention.

"So, I asked Dylan if he had a spare fish to bake for Max. We're heading up to the cheetahs now, and if you like, you can feed it to him."

Standing beneath the platform where the tourists gathered, Lacey was out of sight of anyone who'd come to see the cheetahs up close. Her fingers trembled as she cupped her hands beneath the tinfoil that held the cooked fish. She reached out to the huge, spotted cat that Ryan had assured her was his brother, her heart drumming an erratic tattoo against her ribs.

How the hell is this possible? Please don't let him eat me.

"It's okay, sweetheart. Come on, Max. Step forward."

The cheetah that had been sitting patiently on his haunches watching them now moved forward with a slow, stealth-like grace. Lacey's instincts took over and with a squeal, she dropped the fish and backed away while shaking her hands.

"No, no. I can't."

Her feet danced on the spot, stirring up the dirt beneath her, while her skin was feeling like ants were crawling over every inch of it. Her instincts were still screaming at her to keep running.

The cheetah stared down at the fish she'd dropped and lowered his head, a sad expression passing over his features as he nosed the now dirt covered fish.

She cocked her head as she wondered what he was doing. Why wasn't he eating it?

"Max hates muddy food, sweetheart."

Lacey stilled when a weird, guilty ache settled into her belly as her eyes took in the beautiful animal before her. He was here because of her, and she'd just ruined his treat.

"Oh, I'm so sorry."

Ryan bent down and picked up the fish, carrying it over to a drinking tough where he turned on the tap and doused it with water, being careful to not let any of the muddy water land in the trough.

Lacey shot another quick look at Max to make sure he wasn't going to pounce or anything, and then ran over to Ryan.

"Is that all right now that you've washed it? Can you get all the dirt off? I'm so sorry I dropped it."

She bit her lip and looked back at Max. "Why's he so sad?"

A chuckle erupted from Ryan's beautiful mouth. "Aside from the dirt issue, because we don't really like being in a zoo, Lacey. We're meant to be running wild, chasing animals and drinking healthy, clear water. Being here means we get stared at, have to eat raw, cut up meat we don't catch ourselves, and especially in this enclosure, Max doesn't have any room to run. That's normally the only reason any of us shifters join the coalition here at the zoo, to run free without having to worry about being seen or caught."

Lacey's eyes darted over to the fences, noticing for the first time how small the feeding enclosure was, considering how large the animals were.

For a smaller animal like a dog, it would be a huge yard. But for wild cats it seemed way too small.

"I hadn't thought about it like that. Why don't you guys run somewhere else?"

Ryan frowned and presented the fish to her once more. "Because there is nowhere else in Victoria we won't be spotted, shot, poached or injured. This is it for us, unfortunately. I can't deny my cat and neither can Max, but we'd prefer not to be here. Are you going to try again? I vow to you, he will not hurt you."

She inhaled deeply and stared at the large, cooked fish that had come apart into large pieces now it had been dropped and cleaned up. A twinge of guilt tightened her stomach. She could do this. Really, she could so do this.

"Yes."

She held her palms out, and Ryan settled the tinfoil with the large trout into her hands once again. Lacey noticed the weight and the fragrant smell once more. Even though she'd just eaten, she kind of felt like taking a bite. Turning, she took several steps forward until she was in front of Max again.

"Sorry I dropped it, Max. I'm still a little freaked out by all this shape shifting stuff."

The cheetah lifted his head with a quiet purr before he opened his strong jaws. The beautiful black tear lines running down his face were very prominent from where she now stood.

Her breath stuck in her chest as she allowed Max to eat from her hands. He nibbled on the fish, continuing to purr as he swallowed it piece by piece.

Her heart still raced in her chest, but she began to relax with each gentle tug of Max's powerful teeth. It was like feeding any other domesticated animal by hand, actually even better. She'd had a dog almost bite her once while giving him a treat, but this was just incredible. He was so gentle. The layer of tinfoil also helped boost her confidence. He'd need to bite through that to get to her fingers—not that it would stop him if he wanted to get to her.

Her breath slowed as he got to the final morsels, and she held the tinfoil open allowing him to lick it clean. When the cheeky cat finished, he licked up her inner forearm, and the sandpaper feeling of his rough tongue against her skin had her laughing.

"That really tickles."

She stepped back and grinned at Ryan, who was watching her with a solemn expression.

"Are you all right?"

She grinned as she nodded. She seriously wanted to dance. She bounced over to Ryan and threw her arms around his neck, throwing caution to the wind. "I feel amazing."

She pressed her lips to his, licking at the seam of his mouth, and he opened for her. His tongue dueled with hers while his hands stroked her body, one hand cupping her ass while the other slipped up to her breast, his thumb finding its peak with unerring accuracy.

She gasped and pulled her lips away as her nipples tightening on a dull ache of need.

What the hell was she doing, throwing herself at a man? And in public!

She cleared her throat. "I think that might be enough for now."

She glanced up into his eyes and saw a hunger that she knew he was seeing in hers. Every part of her wanted him to press her up against the wall and remove her clothes as quickly as he could.

"Uh, yeah. I think you might be right. I've got another couple of jobs to do before I finish my shift, so we better head back."

Lacey let Ryan step away, biting her lip as cold air rushed in to replace the warmth that had enveloped her when she'd been in his arms.

He guided her from the feeding yard then as they walked back to the ute, a coldness sweeping through her that left her feeling dejected, like maybe he hadn't wanted the passion she'd thrown at him earlier. Lacey wrapped her arms around herself as she stepped toward her own door, only releasing her hold on herself for the time it took to pull the handle and get herself settled into her seat.

"I'm sorry." The apology was out of her mouth before she could really think about exactly what she was apologizing for.

Ryan paused in reaching to start the engine to turn toward her.

"What on earth for?"

She shrugged, hot tears filling her eyes. She was so confused.

"Hey, hey. What's this all about?"

Her throat ached as she tried to swallow her emotions down, lifting her hands to wipe away the moisture that had fallen onto her cheeks.

"I don't know. I just ... feel ... so strange. And I don't know what you want from me. Was that too much? Me sort of jumping on you?"

Everything was so intense when she was around Ryan or Dylan. She shivered, then pressed her hands to her face as she forced herself to take a shuddering breath.

Ryan started the car and drove away down the track before he pulled off the trail into some scrub, cut the engine and reached for her, his warm hands gripping her chin and turning her towards him.

"You can jump on me anytime, Lacey, but until we've claimed you, it's difficult to control my instincts when you do, so maybe save that for when we're alone, yeah?"

That got a watery sounding chuckle out of her as she relaxed into his hold on her.

"I know this is a lot to take in, Lacey. I can't really imagine what it must be like for you. I've always been a shifter, so it's all second nature to me."

Lacey sobbed, a shaky laugh bursting forth. "I'm actually beginning to love all of the shifter stuff. The cat thing is kinda cool, but it's all happening so fast. Oh, I don't know." Letting out a huge breath, her shoulders sagged, and she stared up at Ryan as her heart ached. "Thanks for being so understanding."

Ryan chuckled, moving forward to press his lips to hers in a gentle kiss that made her reach forward and tangle her fingers in his hair. When they separated, Lacey's heart was thumping against her ribs and her breathing had quickened.

"I ahh…"

Ryan huffed out a laugh. "Yeah, this chemistry is pretty full on, isn't it? Unfortunately, I can't let you come with me for the rest of my shift. How about I drive you back to your car? Or would you like me to find Dylan for you? You could spend the rest of the day with him in the kitchen."

Heat flooded Lacey's face. She couldn't handle fighting her attraction to Dylan after what had just happened with Ryan. "I … think, I might head home for an early night. Although, I still have that article to write, so the early night probably won't happen."

Ryan groaned as she moved back to her seat before he started the vehicle and headed back to the main parking lot.

"Do you know what you're going to write yet?"

Lacey sighed. She'd lain awake half the previous night wondering how she was going to word this damn article.

"I'm not one hundred percent sure just yet. But I promise you, I have zero intention of outing you and your family."

He nodded, and they fell into a comfortable silence for the rest of the short drive back to her car.

"Stay there a sec."

He jumped out of the car and strolled around to her side before he opened the door. With a large hand on her leg, he spun her on the seat so her body faced him. His gaze locked on hers, burning hot with lust, and her legs instinctively spread as he moved to stand between them.

"Just the right height."

He cradled her jaw in his hands and devoured her mouth until her brain went fuzzy and she was having trouble concentrating on the simple act of breathing. He finished the kiss with small nips to her lower lip.

"Enjoy your date with Dylan tomorrow night, beautiful. He'll be picking you up at six from your place. I believe you'll need to dress up for what he has planned."

With her mind still spinning, she struggled to understand what he'd said.

"Right. Dylan. Six tomorrow night. Dress nice. Got it."

With a sexy, deep chuckle, Ryan helped her out of the ute and over to her car like a veritable Prince Charming.

How am I going to survive both of you on Monday night?

Chapter Eleven

"Every woman deserves to be romanced, and even if she won't admit it, she really does want to be swept off her feet."

His mother had been telling Dylan and his brothers that for years. She didn't want her sons getting lazy or thinking they didn't have to work for their mate. Just because they were predestined by Fate to be together, it didn't mean their women were going to fall into their laps. So, it made a strange kind of sense that he had his mother's voice on repeat in his mind as he'd prepared for his date with Lacey tonight.

He glanced to the passenger side of his car. The large floral bunch was a mix of dark pink-centered tiger lilies with smaller white flowers in among them. He'd been planning on simply going for a dozen red roses, but the moment he'd seen this arrangement he'd known it was perfect. He couldn't be boring or predicable when it came to Lacey. She deserved to feel special every step of the way.

But now that he was pulling up into her driveway, he wasn't so sure he'd chosen the right one. What if she thought he was a dick for being so traditional with the whole flower thing?

"Gah!" Dylan tugged at his hair with his fingers. Damn, he hated being nervous. It was as foreign to him as living in the city would be. It was in his nature to just barge in and do whatever needed doing. It was how he was wired. However, nothing he'd ever experienced had made him question his every action and thought like trying to win over Lacey did.

Turning off the ignition, he took a deep breath and let his body settle for a moment. When his muscles stopped quivering, he grabbed the flowers and slid free of the vehicle. His SUV had never looked so spotless. He'd spent most of the day cleaning it inside and out, including a wax and polish of the paintwork. The moment he shut his door, the hairs on the back of his neck tingled. Someone was watching him.

He scanned the area around the front of Lacey's house, narrowing his eyes as he stared into the dark. Deep breaths through his nose helped him to catch any stray scents.

When, after a minute or two of scanning he still couldn't spot anyone, he stalked up to her front door feeling even more uncomfortable than he had when he'd first pulled up.

I should never have agreed to these separate dates.

His brother balanced his extremes out, and he was off-kilter without him by his side. Like this current paranoia that someone was watching him. If Ryan were with him, his twin would simply shake his head on a chuckle, tell him he was mad, and they'd move on with their night.

The door swung in, and Dylan forgot how to breathe. Lacey was a vision in a gorgeous burgundy dress. The neckline was low and came down to a point between her lush breasts, showcasing them to perfection. It came in tight against her until just above her waist where it then flared out a little into a skirt that went all the way to the floor.

Wowza.

"You don't like it? I can change if it's not appropriate for where we're going."

He covered his mouth with a fist as he cleared his throat, shaking his head at her while his eyes did another tour of her body.

"You look amazing, sweetheart. And the dress is perfect for where we're going."

The flowers he held became a weight in his hand, reminding his dazed brain that he had them.

"Um, here. I got these for you."

Damn, he felt ten feet tall when her gaze settled on the pink and white flowers, and she sighed. He'd chosen the right ones. Yes! Then a serene smile lit up her face as she took them from him and buried her nose in among the blooms.

"Oh, these smell divine! Thank you, Dylan. Won't you come in while I get them in some water? Or do we need to get going?"

While he did have a reservation, they had time. He'd been hopeful of sneaking in a kiss or two before they headed off to the restaurant, but now he'd seen her, he didn't think it was a good idea. His imagination took hold, and visions of her voluptuous body swirled through his mind. If he so much as touched her, he wouldn't be able to hold back. He'd have her stripped bare and on the closest flat surface beneath him in seconds.

"We have time, beautiful."

As she turned around and headed off, Dylan stepped inside and closed the door behind him, after he scanned the street once more. That feeling of being watched was still riding him.

"Ry? Are you here?"

When he received no reply, he knew it wasn't his twin out there. Who the hell was watching Lacey's house? Could it be that bastard ex she mentioned? Listening to the sound of running water, Dylan headed into the house but froze as he passed the lounge room.

"Ahh, Lacey? Why's there a gun safe if your lounge room?"

"It's not mine. My roommate, Laura, is a member of the local pistol club. I don't know much about it all as it's never really interested me."

Having been raised on a farm, Dylan had no issue with guns and firearms, but it had been the last thing he'd expected to find in Lacey's house. As he took in the rest of the room, he realized it must be mostly her roommate's things. Nothing in there made him think of Lacey. He continued on to the kitchen where he found Lacey fiddling with the flowers that were now sitting in a large vase.

"Thank you again for these. They're so beautiful."

"Not as beautiful as you, but as close as I could find on such short notice."

She spun and playfully slapped his arm. "Oh, aren't you just oozing charm tonight?"

He wrapped his arm around her waist and pulled her in against him. As he pressed a kiss to the top of her head, he inhaled deeply, savoring her delicate scent that was now tinged with arousal.

"We better get going, sweetheart." Or I'll take you to your room and we won't come back out 'til morning.

Lacey's breath caught in her throat as Dylan's hot body leaned against hers, his hard chest pressing into her shoulder, his groin against her hip. Heat pooled between her thighs as she forced herself to lift her gaze to look at the man making her heart pound like a runaway train. As if he'd been waiting for her to look up, his mouth came crashing down on hers, a growl rumbling in his chest that made the hairs rise on her arms.

He wrapped her in his strong arms and moved her so her front was up against his. She didn't fight against his hold, but instead submitted to him, allowing his passion to sweep her away. She opened her lips to his seeking tongue as her eyes slid closed. Lacey moaned as his hands gripped her ass and pulled her flush against him. Their tongues dueled as their kiss deepened.

Another deep rumble rose from Dylan, and he pulled away from her, his brown eyes sparkling with fire as his breath labored in out of his heaving chest.

"Fuck, you're hot."

A chuckle broke free as she tried to push down the heat that was racing up her neck and over her cheeks. The fact such a delicious specimen of a man thought she was hot had her head spinning and her knees weak. So much for him playing the gentleman tonight.

"Uh ... you're not too bad yourself. I'll just grab my coat, and we can get going."

She turned and bolted to her bedroom as fast as she could manage on her now wobbly legs. Three dates. Her demand had seemed like a great idea at the time, but now she was tempted to throw in the towel and pull Dylan into her bedroom. She was grateful he'd knocked it down from the original six she'd demanded. No way would she have been able to hold out that long.

She grabbed her long black coat and slipped it on before pausing for a minute to take some deep breaths in an attempt to calm her heart rate down. It wasn't too cold outside, so she didn't bother doing her coat up. A quick glance in her full-length mirror had her smiling. Even she had to admit she filled out her new dress well, which she'd bought this morning just for tonight.

Still smiling, she strode back into the lounge. There were little fissions of excitement bubbling though her veins. She hadn't felt this happy in a long time, and she was struggling not to squeal like a little girl.

Her fingers trembled as she picked up her bag and stepped towards her gorgeous date. Dylan's sexual vibe was so intense it stole the breath from her lungs for a few moments.

"Let's go, shall we?"

Dylan nodded at her as he spoke, and he followed her out onto the porch. She stopped abruptly with a gasp as the hairs the back of her neck stood to attention. Dylan ran into her with a grunt but grabbed her around the waist and managed to prevent them both from tripping down her front stairs face first.

"What's wrong?"

"Someone's watching us."

Her neck continued to prickle as her gaze darted from her car in the driveway to the hedges by the house. Where is the bastard hiding this time?

"I agree. I felt the same thing when I pulled up, but I couldn't see anyone. Then or now."

An icy shiver snaked down her spine as Dylan's comment pushed aside any belief she was simply being paranoid. Dylan's warm body pressed closer. "You okay, sweetheart?"

Lacey nodded and swallowed hard, as a sense of being trapped had claustrophobia swamping her mind and soul. Her throat was suddenly tight, and her heart thumped against her ribs. Nausea rolled through her, and she grabbed at Dylan's hands that lay against her aching stomach.

"If you want, I can shift and track whoever it is down."

Dylan's whispered words broke through her panic, and Lacey blinked back to reality as she turned her head towards her date. Her whole body relaxed, the tension in her shoulders draining away. Stupid panic attack. She was standing with a powerful cheetah shifter. She was safe. The cold coil in her gut warmed and vanished as though it had never been.

She forced a smile to her lips and shook her head. "No, but thank you. Whoever it is doesn't deserve our energy or time. I'd much rather head out and enjoy our dinner."

They stepped towards his car, and he dashed forward, opening the door for her. Wow, and I'd thought you'd be the less romantic one.

"Well, thank you, kind sir."

She battled the urge to laugh and slid into the comfortable car, putting on her seat belt as her gaze strayed to the hedges once again. She couldn't shake the sensation that someone was there and unfortunately, she knew precisely who it would be. Please let him be gone by the time we get back.

"So, who would be watching you?" Dylan pulled shut his door and started the car.

She winced. "My ex. Probably."

Dylan frowned at her, then returned his focus to reversing out of her drive before he started driving towards the city.

"Why would you assume that? Has he been giving you trouble lately?"

She rolled her eyes. "You saw his text message. He wants us to get back together, while I obviously don't. He's gotten a little obsessed and honestly, I'm not sure what to do about it."

A rumble filled the car, and she turned to face Dylan with wide eyes.

"Was that you growling?"

Dylan gave her a strained look, his face pulling down into a frown.

"Sorry, but the bullshit your ex is pulling isn't just pissing me off, but riling up my cheetah too."

Unsure how to handle these men's protective sides, she looked down and studied her nails for a moment. Time for a subject change.

"So, where are we going tonight?"

"Well..." Dylan gave her a gorgeous smile, and her own lips lifted to mirror the expression. "I thought you'd like a nice dinner out. So, I'm wining and dining you, sweetheart."

She laughed as she clenched her thighs, squeezing them together in the hopes of curbing the excitement building within her. "Trying to get into my pants, huh, big boy?"

"Always, babe. Or under your skirt in this case."

With a grin, she settled into her seat, loving how Dylan made her feel. They traveled for some time in comfortable silence, the city lights flying by as she relaxed her head against the head rest.

When the car began to slow, she started paying more attention. Dylan pulled up outside a restaurant Lacey didn't recognize. Through the large front windows, she could see tables set with crisp white linen, romantic looking candles in the center of each one.

She gasped and leaned closer to the window. "Oh, I'm even more excited now." And really glad I dressed up as much as I did.

She hopped out to the sound of Dylan muttering something about her making it difficult for him to be a gentleman when she rushed to get out of the car all the damn time. With a wide grin, she looked to Dylan as he came up beside her on the sidewalk, where he tilted his elbow toward her as he bowed slightly. With a wide grin, she wound her arm through his and allowed him to lead the way.

She was still smiling as they walked into the beautiful, candlelit restaurant, where they were greeted with gentle music that completed the perfect atmosphere.

An elegant, middle-aged man in black dress pants and a white shirt with a black tie greeted them with old-world manners that left Lacey gobsmacked. She hadn't realized men like that existed anymore. By the time she got over the shock, they'd been seated at a table near a large window that showed a stunning view over the Yarra River.

"Dylan, this is beautiful."

His smile lit up the room and instantly had her focusing only on him.

"It's pretty cool, isn't it? I've heard great things about the head chef here, and I have high expectations for what we'll eat tonight."

She picked up the leather-bound menu and let her eyes wander down the list. Nothing jumped out at her, and she went out so rarely, she wasn't sure what to choose. She was more than happy for Dylan to take the lead with their food.

"Maybe you could guide me on what to order then, because I'm not sure where to even start with this menu."

"Want me to order for you?"

She raised her eyebrows as she stared at his expectant face. Why not?

She placed the menu down and grinned over at him.

"That would be wonderful. I'm not overly fond of fish, but other than that, do your worst."

He clapped his hands before rubbing them together with a fiendish laugh. "Brilliant."

When a waiter approached, Dylan sat taller while he cleared his throat. She smiled with a chuckle as his excitement permeated the air around them.

Lacey glanced around the room at the elegantly dressed ladies and gentlemen. A sigh escaped her throat when her gaze caught on a beautiful woman in red. She adored bright colors but was far too self-conscious of her size to risk wearing them. Dylan's deep voice kept grabbing her attention even though she was doing her best to block out what he was saying. She wanted to be surprised when her meal arrived.

Dylan slid his hand over hers, gaining her full attention quickly.

"Lacey, would you like a glass of wine?"

"Yes, please. A sauvignon blanc, if possible."

The waiter bowed slightly before turning away, and Lacey reached for the bread roll on her plate and tore it in half. She started to lift a piece to her lips, then put it down again as she glanced around again at the other customers. Was it bad etiquette to eat bread with your fingers in an upscale restaurant? Who cares? Lifting the bread once more, she took a bite and nearly moaned at how good the freshly baked roll tasted. It was so delicious she couldn't help but pick up another piece. Bad luck if Dylan or anyone else here didn't like her using her fingers.

He gave her a smirk but stayed silent.

Butterflies took flight in her belly as she swallowed and smiled. "So, what's Ryan doing tonight?"

"Sitting in front of the TV sulking about missing out on having dinner with you, I suspect."

Lacey's heart ached in her chest as Ryan's face swam before her eyes. She'd deliberately left him out. Oh, crap. It had never been her intention to hurt either of these sweet men. She'd just wanted to get to know each of them better.

"That's terrible. Should we call him and invite him to join us?"

He waved his hand in the air, "No, don't be ridiculous. It's my night."

Lacey opened her mouth to tell Dylan how childish he was being, but then shut it again. Wasn't this her idea? She'd asked them to split up to date her. She was the one who had convinced herself she'd need to choose between them. But did she ... could she? They certainly seemed all for sharing her.

Grateful for the distraction, she gave the waiter her full attention when he arrived and served their wine with one hand behind his back and a flourish that was just perfect for a glitzy night out.

She lifted her glass and pushed down the rising quiver in her belly. She didn't need to make a choice yet, and she wasn't going to rush herself into making a decision.

"To first dates."

Dylan grinned and held up his own drink filled with blood-red wine.

"To forever."

The vehemence in his voice made her throat sting and her eyes tingle. He was completely serious.

She blinked and leaned forward to clink their glasses together before raising it to her lips to take a drink. She barely withheld a groan as she swallowed the cool liquid down her throat. Fruity flavor and a crisp aftertaste had her rolling her tongue around her mouth to fully appreciate the taste.

Before she could take another mouthful, a bowl was placed in front of her, and wafts of creamy cheese and apricot curled up her nostrils.

"Since you said no fish, I went with filo pastry wrapped around fried apricots and brie. Sound good?"

Oh, hell yes.

Lacey picked up her fork and set her wine down.

"Absolutely.

****

Ryan never should have agreed to separate dates. They were two halves of a whole, and there was no way Lacey was having a good time with only one of them there with her. Dylan needed him to soften his edges. His twin had a nasty habit of just barging into a situation with no care or finesse, let alone any thought to how it could go wrong. Damn, but he hoped Lacey was still talking to them by the end of the night.

He glanced at his watch again. Nine-thirty. Surely, they weren't still at the restaurant? Or had Dylan broken through with Lacey and managed to get her into bed? He shook the thought from his mind. No way. His twin would have contacted him to get his ass to her house if he'd managed to seduce her.

Well, if he knows what's good for him, he would.

With a frustrated growl, he scrubbed his hands over his face. No, his first thought was right. His twin may be hot-headed, but when it came to their mate, Dylan wouldn't be selfish. At least this was the final time they'd have to do things separately. Tomorrow night ended this stupid "let me date you separately" thing. Damn, he hoped she wasn't going to try to choose just one of them. How on earth would they get around that? Could he step aside to allow his twin happiness with their mate? Could Dylan?

No fucking way. I'd rather sit on a cactus.

With a groan, he shook his head and headed to the fridge for a beer. Even if she did think she could choose between them, he and Dylan knew better. They'd grown up knowing about the mate bond and had always prepared themselves for the reality that they would most likely share a woman. And now that they knew Lacey was their mate? None of them, least of all Lacey, would feel complete without the other two. Grabbing the bottle opener, Ryan popped the top off and took a long drink. Cold hops slid down his throat, helping relieve some of the burn inside his chest.

Besides, they had plans for their little mate. Plans that would cure her of ever wanting to be parted from either of them. Ryan hoped she wouldn't need too long to agree to commit to them. He knew humans didn't normally do things as quickly as they intended to, but now he'd found his mate, he didn't want to be away from her side.

The sound of an engine coming up the drive had Ryan gunning for the front door. He stood on the front porch tapping his foot on the wooden deck while he waited for his twin, who took his sweet time getting out of his car.

"What happened? How'd it go?"

The wide grin on his twin's puss was a good sign things had gone well, and some of the tension drained out of Ryan's tight shoulders. He really hoped Dylan hadn't said something completely stupid and ruined their chances.

"Lacey is one of a kind, brother."

Dylan was going to drive him insane.

"I already know that. What happened?"

Dylan stepped closer, rolling his eyes as he practically swooned on the steps.

"And you should have seen the dress she was wearing tonight. Fucking hell, she is hot!"

Ryan clenched his free hand into a fist at his side and resisted the urge to grab Dylan by the expensive shirt collar and haul him into the house.

"That she is. Now stop fucking with me and tell me what happened!"

His twin had the gall to laugh.

"Ry, you are so easy to rile up some days. I didn't fuck things up. We're still on for tomorrow night. If the way she moaned while I had my tongue down her throat was any indication, she's perfectly happy with how our date went."

Some things would never change. Ryan shook his head on a sigh.

"Seriously, Dylan, Lacey is our mate, not some slutty hook-up. Talk about her with some respect, would you?"

With another eye roll, Dylan stormed up the stairs and into the house. Ryan turned to follow him, sipping his beer as he walked behind him. Once his twin made it to the kitchen and grabbed his own drink, he turned back to face Ryan with a serious expression that had Ryan's instincts flaring. Ryan didn't like that look one bit. It meant that something had happened.

"You said you didn't stuff things up. Was that a lie?"

Dylan was crass and harsh, but he was always honest. He stared at his twin a little longer, tapping into his brother's feelings and getting a wave of hot anger and unease for his efforts. He shivered in response. This wasn't good.

"No lie. We're good. But Lacey's in danger. When I got to her house, someone was watching nearby. She said she could sense someone was watching us too. She tried to brush it off, saying it was just her ex and not to worry, but that was utter bullshit. We need to go out and find that bastard and take care of him. You know that now he's seen me with her, he'll be jealous as hell. Asshole will probably do something stupid sooner rather than later."

Ryan forced his body to stay still. Fury and possessiveness were pushing him to shift and go to Lacey right now. His skin was tingling, and his cheetah was emerging from his subconscious like a jack-in-the-box. Both wanted to make sure she was safe and protected.

"Do we need to go now? Was he there when you got back?"

Dylan shook his head.

"No, I did a sweep before I left to make sure. No one was there. And her roommate has a bloody gun safe in the lounge room. The woman is a member of a pistol club, and guess what Lacey's planning to do with her day tomorrow?" Dylan smirked and took a drink before continuing, "She and Laura are having a nice relaxing day at home. Together."

Ryan couldn't stop the quirk at the edges of his lips as he imagined Lacey learning some self-defense techniques. "Okay, so that gives us some time to track this bastard down. Don't suppose you got his name or any other details, did you?"

His twin's shoulders slumped. "Nope. All I have is his phone number from that first night. She's never once called him by a real name."

Ryan's mind began racing through options. What was the fastest way for them to track him down?

"Don't suppose you know if Eli's on nightshift tonight?"

Dylan's shoulder rose in a half shrug as he took another mouthful of his beer.

"Only one way to find out."

Setting down his now empty bottle, Ryan pulled his mobile out and scrolled down to the number of the local police station. Eli was the eldest of the lion boys and the best of the lot, in Ryan's opinion. He'd always gone out of his way to make sure that everyone knew he didn't care about the whole lions vs. cheetahs' rivalry. Ryan prayed that meant he'd help them out with protecting their mate. He also hoped like hell the man was working tonight and they could get on with the job of protecting Lacey.

CHAPTER TWELVE

Lacey reached out and caught the bag of salt and vinegar chips Laura threw at her, laughing as her best friend dropped down onto the couch next to her.

"What movie did you choose?"

In answer to Laura's question, Lacey picked up the two romantic comedies she hadn't been able to choose between. She wanted to zone out with some mindless laughs and love. Laura loved her old-school DVD player and refused to watch any of the streaming services. Since she also had a massive collection of DVDs, Lacey hadn't ever tried to change her mind.

"I got it down to these two but can't decide which one. You pick."

Laura looked between them for a minute then hopped up to put whichever one she'd decided on in the DVD player and grabbed the remote.

Lacey sighed and settled back into the comfortable old leather couch. She picked up her phone once again and pressed the screen so that it would light up. Nothing. It had been an hour since Ryan had messaged and she wanted to hear from him—or Dylan—again. She frowned in disappointment as a heaviness set into her chest. Which was plain crazy. She couldn't believe she was so affected by these men. She shook her head and forced away the negative thoughts. She was going to have a relaxing day with her bestie. No men allowed. Or thoughts of men. No matter how hot they were. And they were damn hot.

Laura reached forward to grab a couple of Cokes from the coffee table and after opening them both, handed one to Lacey. They really were having a pig-out today, and really, why not?

"What are you frowning about, Lace?"

Lacey tossed her phone onto a pillow further down the couch so she wouldn't look at it again.

"I keep looking at my phone to see if Ryan has messaged. I'm being ridiculous."

Laura shrugged and bit into a salt and vinegar chip. "You're not. I'm glad you're finally having some fun after all the stress your fuck-wit ex has put you through."

Lacey shivered and looked away. So much for no thinking of men today. She definitely didn't want to be wasting time on her ex. She'd been an idiot to date him in the first place, and now she was paying the price.

No... concentrate on my new men. Yes... Dylan and Ryan.

If we were going to talk men, Lacey figured she might as well get her friend's take on her new situation.

"Yeah, I agree. But it's not necessarily just fun."

Laura turned to face her. "What? You haven't fucked him yet?"

Lacey whacked her best friend in the arm and grabbed the bag of M & Ms out of her lap, stuffing a small handful of the chocolates in her mouth to distract herself from the fire leaping across her cheeks.

Laura cocked an eyebrow at her. "What?"

She glared at her crass friend. Laura was the most indelicate person she knew.

"No, I haven't slept with them yet. Don't be ridiculous."

"Them? Who's them? I thought his name was Ryan."

Acid pooled in Lacey's gut as she stared at her hands. If she wanted Laura's help with what to do, she was going to have to be brave and fess up. And hope she didn't react badly. She swallowed around the lump in her throat. "Uh, I had a date with Dylan last night and Ryan the day before."

"What? You're dating two men? Do they know about each other?"

Lacey forced herself to lift her head despite the rawness in her throat and the tightness in her chest. She had to answer Laura's questions, and heaven help her if Laura was as horrified as Lacey feared she might be.

"They're identical twins and they both want to date me, so I kinda am."

Laura's face lit up, and she let out a whoop of delight.

"Oh, girl, that is awesome! You guys gonna do a threesome or what?"

Lacey buried her face in her hands at the sight of Laura's huge grin and sparkling eyes. Trust her to confide in the only woman she knew who would see the bright side of the situation.

She answered through her hands, "Yeah, something like that."

"I'm jealous now ... wow! That is super cool."

Lacey exhaled and let her hands drop. She felt drained, and her muscles ached. She'd finally told someone about her weird conundrum, and Laura was totally for it. Of course, Lacey hadn't explained the whole cheetah thing or the mate for life part, but Laura didn't need to know everything.

"So, when are you seeing them next?"

"Well, we're meant to have a date tomorrow night but..."

"You want to see them tonight?"

Lacey swallowed hard and nodded. "Yeah, kinda."

She missed them. Dylan's heat, Ryan's calm. Their handsome faces and tender kisses. She let her shoulders slump.

"I'm pathetic."

"No, you're not. I need to run to the loo, so you message them and set up a date for tonight and when I get back, we can watch the movie and then pick out a super hot outfit for you."

Lacey snorted, which made her laugh, her heart lifting in hope that the relationship that was blossoming between her and the boys could actually work.

"Okay."

Laura jumped up and headed off to the bathroom, and Lacey grabbed her phone just as a message came in from Dylan.

Had a great time last night. Miss you.

A squeal rose in her throat, and she took a deep breath to calm her nerves.

She was going to see them again soon. Yes!

She typed a message back.

I miss you too. Can the three of us catch up tonight for a bit?

She held her phone to her chest and bit her lip. A ding sounded and she opened the message.

Absolutely. Wanna come to our place, or can we drop in there?

She weighed her options. She had to work in the morning so going to their place would be silly, plus she wasn't sure she wanted to head out alone tonight. She couldn't put her finger on why not, but she just knew it was a bad idea.

Would love you to come here. And this doesn't change tomorrow night, right?

She hoped it didn't affect their final date. She wanted to see them tomorrow too.

We have big plans for tomorrow night, nothing will change that. Okay, we have a few things to do this afternoon, but we'll drop over about eight to see you tonight. Does that work?

She answered straight away.

Yes, perfect. See you then.

A squeal left her lips, and Laura walked back into the room.

"All good?"

She nodded and grinned up at her roommate. "Yeah, they're coming over after dinner for a while."

Her arms now tingled with electricity and energy.

"Well, then we have all day to get you ready."

Laura held up a bottle of hot red nail polish and Lacey sighed, her mood lighter than it had been all day. Yes, they did have all day, and when the boys arrived that night, she would be ready.

"Do you think Eli will have much for us?"

Dylan winced at Ryan's question that mirrored his own thoughts.

"I seriously hope so, brother. He's going to do something soon. I can feel it in the pit of my stomach."

Turning away from his twin, he pushed through the front door of the Matong Police Station, relishing the blast of cool air. Victoria was cooler than the more northern states of Australia, but late January was bloody hot no matter where you were Down Under.

"Morning, boys. Eli mentioned you might be in looking for him today. Come on through."

The beauty of living in a rural community was that everyone knew who you were. Of course, that wasn't always a good thing, but on days like today it sure was.

"Thanks, Jimmy."

Dylan fell into his usual place behind his twin as they followed Jimmy through the back part of the station. Eli was a detective so had a small office rather than a desk out in the open with the other officers. Jimmy knocked on the open door before he called out to Eli.

"Hey, man, Dylan and Ryan are here for you. You right to see them now?"

Eli looked up from where he'd been frowning at his computer, a small smile tugging at his lips as he saw them.

"Thanks, Jimmy. Come on in, boys."

Eli stood and moved toward them. He closed the door behind Jimmy before shaking each of their hands.

"I'm guessing you don't want to waste time shooting the breeze, so take a seat and we'll get down to it."

Nervous energy filled the room, and Dylan's palms grew damp as his mind spun with possibilities.

Ryan leaned forward in his seat. "So, you had some luck finding information then?"

"Okay, first, this is all strictly off the books. It sure as hell isn't legal for me to check into a civilian and then pass that information on to other civilians. So, you two are not to go running off half-cocked with this information and do something stupid. Understand? By coming to me, you're including me in your situation—which I damn straight appreciate— and it also means you're going to listen to my information and my advice about what needs to happen. Is that clear?"

Dylan followed Ryan's hoarse "Of course" with one of his own. He'd do his best to follow Eli's instructions, but Lacey was their mate. He'd do anything to keep her safe.

"Right. Now, you both believe your mate is in danger. I'm assuming Dylan was with you last night when you rang me, Ryan?"

"Of course, so yes, he knows what I've told you about all the things that have gone on."

"Good. The thing that concerns me most—well, aside from the overly possessive tone of his messages to Lacey—is that both Dylan and Lacey felt that they were being watched at her place. I know any human would write it off as nothing more than their imagination, but we know better, don't we? With that in mind, I dug up what I could. His name is Rodney Dobson, and he's thirty-two years old. I know full well what you'll both do with his address, so I'll keep that to myself but I've put his street on the list for regular drive-bys so the local cops will see if he does anything out of the ordinary at home. He works three blocks away from his home. He's the manager of a McDonalds restaurant."

"So, he's a big fish in a little pond then?"

Dylan nodded with his twin's assessment.

"That's a good way to put it. He's never tried to move up from being the manager, and he's been there for years. I'd say he enjoys having people do what he tells them. He'd relish putting together the roster."

Ryan snorted. "No doubt giving people the most inconvenient shifts possible."

Dylan mentally shook his head. What kind of asshole got his kicks out of making teenagers' lives difficult? The same kind that wouldn't allow a woman to leave him on her terms.

"His official record is nothing out of the ordinary. A couple speeding fines and parking tickets. There's no indication that he's ever gotten violent with a partner. That said, a lot of victims of domestic violence don't come forward, so just because he doesn't have a record doesn't mean he's been a saint in the past, by any means."

Dylan rubbed the back of his neck. What a mess. "So—legally speaking— we can't do anything, can we?"

"Lacey could get a restraining order against him, but honestly, I doubt that will make a lick of difference to this guy's behavior. Unfortunately, we can't arrest him until he actually does something illegal."

Ryan turned from Eli to face him.

"We're going there tonight, but I doubt she'll be inviting us to stay over every night. We need to keep her protected. She'll be at work during the day but in the evening, we need to be there in case he pulls something."

"We'll talk to Dad and get our shifts moved around at the zoo, then take turns in the evenings keeping an eye on her and her place."

"But neither of you can go jumping him even if he is there watching her. You have to call me in if anything happens."

Dylan spoke before Ryan could, "Neither of us will stand by if she's in danger. You know she's our mate, and you understand why we can't not protect her."

"Calm down, Dylan. If Rodney makes a move to hurt Lacey, that's a different story. You can defend her if she's in danger, but him passively watching her house is not causing her harm. I need your word that you'll ring me if you find him there. Promise me that the first thing you'll do upon finding Rodney will be to call me."

He was unable to contain it. A growl left Dylan's chest, earning him a thump from Ryan and a scowl from Eli.

"You have my and Dylan's word that we'll contact you first."

"If there's time."

Eli sighed. "I guess that's as good as I'm going to get. Go on, get out of here and go protect your woman."

CHAPTER THIRTEEN

She was really doing this.

What she was doing exactly, she wasn't entirely sure. But as all sorts of ideas popped into her mind, she paced her lounge room and shook out her hands, alternatively squealing and groaning as indecision warred within her.

She'd started the weekend with the problem of having to choose between two handsome and different men. Now she was trying to justify her desire for both, and was actually considering their ludicrous plan to share her.

Was that even possible?

A car pulled up in her driveway, the rumble of the engine and lights through the window making her run to the front door. Her stomach was filled with butterflies and her hands trembled, slipping as she tried to grip the door handle.

She'd never done anything so crazy as this before, and she bit her lip as she tried to focus on getting the damn door open. She didn't care how crazy what she was doing would sound to anyone else. Laura had convinced her to throw caution to the wind and live it up. What did she have to lose?

She finally managed to pull the open the door and froze to watch the men prowl up toward the house. They were a marvel to see, their fluid grace and cheeky smiles reminiscent of the powerful animals they'd turned into. Her breath caught in her throat. That was something else she had to consider, but she'd worry about that side of things later.

"Hey."

She melted against the door as they rushed up to her. Then they somehow managed to pull her inside and get the door shut within seconds.

Her mind was spinning when Dylan pushed her up against the closest wall and her legs turned to jelly as he growled against her throat like the beautiful cat he was. He laid his lips against hers as he cupped her jaw with one palm, while his other slid down to her ass. He was so passionate and needy, and she couldn't believe how much she wanted him.

"Dylan, she said she wanted to talk." Ryan's calm voice laced with humor pulled Lacey up and out of her heated fog, Dylan moving off her with a frustrated sigh.

"No." She grabbed at his shirt and pulled him back to her. Dylan had read her intentions right. "I want this, please."

Dylan's voice dropped to a low rumble. "Where's your bedroom?"

She took his hand and pulled him towards the door off the lounge that led to her bedroom. She hoped Ryan was right behind them.

She pushed open the door, her breathing coming in pants as Dylan stepped close, the heat of his body pressing through their clothes and imprinting on her skin.

"Where's Ryan?"

She looked around her darkened bedroom where she'd lit several candles, hoping to see that he'd got past them somehow. Nothing.

She twisted away from Dylan and poked her head back into the lounge to see her lovely man loitering around the couch.

"What are you doing?"

He looked up, his cheeks flushed with heat. "I wasn't sure whether you wanted me or if I should go. I..."

Her heart broke a little for her gentle man. *I'm so sorry, Ryan. I shouldn't have made you guys think I'd choose between you.*

She held out her hand and smiled at him, injecting as much warmth into her gaze as she could.

"I want you both."

His lips lifted into a huge smile, and he jogged across the room to her.

She stood up on her tiptoes and lifted her lips to him, wanting to reassure him that she did want him. She wanted them both. Ryan pressed into her, his sweet taste spreading across her tongue and warming her to the core.

When he finally pulled away, her knees were weak, and she staggered back until she sat down on her mattress with a contented sigh.

Ryan shut the door, and the metal latch clicked into place.

"Are you ready to mate with us?" Dylan asked her, his tone gruff as he stood next to her bed.

Not yet... please don't force me to make that decision just yet.

She shook her head, swallowing hard against the uncomfortable pain in her chest. "I don't think I'm ready for that yet, but I wanted a little more time with you both. To kiss you, touch you. We barely get to spend any time together."

The brothers shared a look and then nodded, stepping forward as one.

"Let's make sure you get your kisses then, beautiful."

Dylan pulled her to her feet and began tugging at her clothes.

She helped him pull off her blouse, and she stepped out of her sandals and skirt.

"I thought you were hot in that dress you wore on our date, but naked? Damn, woman."

His words would have made her laugh if his gaze hadn't been so heated, scanning her from head to toe. No one had ever said she was hot before.

Ryan's hands came around her waist, his warm lips touching her neck as his fingers traced patterns over her hips.

Tingles of pleasure radiated out from her core as she ignored the feelings of inadequacy hitting her. She was bigger than what society said was normal, but the candlelight was the most flattering and the men didn't seem put off by her yet.

"You are ... so beautiful..." Ryan's words rumbled into her ear, and she let her eyes close, giving in to the atmosphere of contentment and happiness that was sweeping her away. She'd never felt so loved before, even with her past long-term boyfriends. It made no sense that she'd already fallen so hard and fast, but these men fulfilled every ache of her heart.

Ryan's hands unclipped her bra and it slid down her arms and onto the floor.

Dylan dropped lower, his lips capturing one nipple in his mouth, and she cried out as he tugged hard.

Her head fell back on Ryan's shoulder, and she arched her back, threading her fingers into the short hair at Dylan's nape as he suckled on her.

"Let's move this to the bed. Lie down, beautiful."

Ryan's words floated around her as she forced open her eyes. She stepped over to her bed and crawled on before turning over and reaching for them. She wanted them closer. They were too far away now.

Dylan pulled off his t-shirt, while Ryan climbed between her thighs. Still fully dressed, the denim of his jeans brushed over her sensitive skin, making her shiver.

"I have dreamed about you like this, how you would smell, how you would taste."

He pressed soft kisses to her stomach and then stopped to suckle each breast, his hands plumping up the flesh and arousing her moans.

She arched and grabbed for him with one hand, reaching out the other for Dylan, who slid down onto the bed minus his shirt but still clothed in his jeans.

"Why aren't you both stripping off?" she asked as he moved closer. Why couldn't she have them as bare as she was?

"If we can't take you tonight, I think it's best we don't get naked. I doubt I'd be able to control myself if I did."

She looked down her body as Ryan moved back and pulled her knickers with him.

She lifted up and let him totally disrobe her.

"That's not fair, Dylan. I should give you both pleasure too."

Dylan chuckled and wrapping his palm around her hip moved her so she lay on her side, facing him.

"Oh, this will be our pleasure, don't you worry."

His hand slid between her thighs, and she opened for him as he kissed her.

Ryan moved onto the bed behind her and pressed his naked chest to her back, a wave of rightness, of belonging, flowing over her.

She cried out as Dylan's fingers grazed her clit, sending out pulsing waves of need.

She arched back and turned her head, Ryan capturing her mouth as Dylan's mouth attached to her nipple and pulled hard.

Her mind whirled around like a storming sea as she was being seduced from every side.

Dylan's fingers moved away, and his twin took up his place. Ryan's hand moved over her hip, dipping between her spread legs and slid a finger into her wet pussy.

She clamped down on him and moaned into his mouth as her body ached harder for them.

Ryan kept kissing her as Dylan played with the flesh of her breasts and her tight nipples. Ryan alternated between swirling wet fingers around her throbbing clit and then dipping them into her aching channel.

"Ugh, fuck..." She broke off from Ryan's mouth to pant and stare down her body to the incredible imagery of two men's hands working her flesh, their intent and purpose to pleasure her.

That, alone, was enough to push her close to the edge.

Her belly tightened and her pussy clenched down on his fingers, that throbbing aching intensifying to the point that she could hear her heart beating loudly in her ears.

"Oh, yes. Good girl."

"Dylan, lick her clit for me."

Dylan gave her a wicked smile as he slid down her body and pushed her back, so she was practically lying on Ryan.

Ryan slid a second finger into her, and she arched as crackles of tension exploded around her.

Dylan put his head between her thighs and set his tongue on her clit.

"Oh ... God! Dylan!"

He flicked her clit from side to side, and Ryan's fingers moved faster, fucking her harder.

She reached for them, digging her nails into each of them as the tension in her body built higher and tighter.

"Come on, Lacey. Come for us, beautiful."

She panted and cried out, heading towards that climax before the abyss. Her legs straightened, and she grabbed at her men, the coil inside her tightening to the point of breaking.

Dylan was moaning as he ate at her, and Ryan sucked on her neck as she reached the point of no return. The breath caught in her throat, and then it hit her. Her pussy grabbed at Ryan's fingers, and waves of pleasure rolled through her as her body began to shudder in their arms.

She screamed and let the white lights take her, her spasming body crying out in bliss.

When she swam back up through the heated ocean surrounding her, Dylan and Ryan were still there, touching her, kissing her, soothing her still shuddering body.

"Thank you. Thank you so much."

She collapsed against them and snuggled into their warmth, her need for these men becoming more and more concrete in her mind.

"Should we go?" Ryan asked her, kissing the side of her neck.

"No, please don't."

She tried to open her eyes but every time she did, they were so blurry, her brain forced her to slam them shut again.

Her desire to stay conscious was losing the fight with sleep, a strange, heavy lethargy swimming in to drag her down.

"We both have to work early, but we'll stay until sunrise, okay?"

Dylan began to move away, and she grabbed for him.

"Just stripping down to boxers, sweetheart."

"Oh, all right."

Both men slid out of bed, and her belly dropped with the coldness of losing them.

She shuffled onto her side and held her breath, consciousness now more appealing.

She didn't want to miss any more time with them.

They slid back beneath the sheets and reached for her, their synchronicity and perfect rhythm making tears swim in her eyes. To be the focus of these men's attentions was more than a dream come true, it was a fantasy she'd never had the courage to dream of.

"Goodnight, beautiful girl."

"Goodnight, Ryan. Goodnight, Dylan. Thank you both. That was absolutely incredible."

They each kissed her gently on the lips and then settled beside her.

She blinked back the tears and let herself settle into the soft mattress and the hard muscles of the men around her.

"When will I see you again?"

Dylan purred in front of her. "Tomorrow night."

"Good."

She didn't hear them leave, but her body ached from their loving long after they departed for work, letting her know they'd been really here with her.

How dare she! Who did that little bitch think she was to flaunt not one but two men in front of him like that? Rodney slammed his car door in a vain attempt to vent some of his fury. She was his. Only his. She did not belong with those two pretty boys who'd been hanging around her skirts for the past week.

He'd had to put some serious time into getting into Lacey's pants. She'd played hard to get and made him work for her, something that she was not demanding of her new men.

Of course, he'd made the most of it when he finally did get the goods. She'd been so fucking hot, and he wanted her again. It didn't make sense that when they'd finally gotten to the good stuff, she'd started backing away from him. But those pretty boys had been at her for less than a week and already they had her horizontal.

Slut.

He'd had to leave. He couldn't stand watching their silhouettes through her curtains a minute longer. The plan had been to approach her tonight. She must have changed her phone number again as she wasn't answering his texts or his calls anymore. If he could just speak with her, make her see how well they suited each other, it would all work out. He could ease up on the rough stuff between the sheets ... for a while, at least.

After taking a deep breath, he slid his key home and opened his front door. Before he stepped inside, a car drove past slowly, and he turned to see it was a cop car. What the fuck? That was the third patrol car he'd seen in the last twenty-four hours. He frowned. Had Lacey reported him? Or was it her new toy boys? As the vehicle left his line of sight, he turned back toward his house. He was going to have to really watch himself when he left to go to her place from now on.

His place was dark. He hated coming home to an empty house. Another reason he needed Lacey back. He needed her here, waiting for him with dinner cooking and her soft body ready to ease his needs.

He strode down the hallway without turning on any lights. He had to see her. He flipped the switch as he crossed into their bedroom. He had it all set up for her return, including every photo he had of them together and several of her on her own that he'd taken from her social media before she'd blocked him. Until he had her back in person, these images of her enjoying her life would have to take her place. He flopped down on the bed and looked at the largest image he had of her. It was a photo her trigger-happy housemate had taken of her. She was outside with the wind blowing her blonde hair around her happy, smiling face. He'd had the photo enlarged as big as he could get the photo place to do it ... nearly life-size.

"Why'd you have to invite them over tonight, babe?"

He was on late shifts for the rest of the week. With her working days at the paper, he wouldn't get a chance to see her again until Friday night. He would have to make sure that he got to speak with her then. He frowned as he stared at her lush mouth. Yes, he would make certain he got some face-to-face time with his girl Friday night. Still focused on those lips that had felt so fucking good wrapped around his dick, he loosened the fly on his pants. As he slipped his palm around his hard, aching cock, he closed his eyes and imagined it was her hand on him. Pleasuring him.

Dylan rolled his shoulder as he got out his car and headed toward his house. The restaurant at the zoo had been flat out all day. Add that to how he'd spent the previous night, and he was so fucking tired he could pass out where he stood. Not that he was complaining, of course. Well, okay, so maybe he was complaining just a little. As much as he'd loved lying beside Lacey watching her sleep all night, he had the worst case of blue balls he'd ever experienced as a reward.

He trudged inside to find Ryan with his head in the fridge, wearing nothing but a towel.

"Grab me a beer too, would you?"

Ryan turned and handed one off to him. "Here you go. Figured you'd be looking for one."

"Is that why you're out here in a towel? To get me a beer?" Dylan didn't believe it for a second.

"We need to talk, and I wanted to catch you before you had your shower."

Yeah, because he intended to have a long one in an attempt to ease some of the ache in his cock. His twin knew him well enough to know that, and Dylan didn't doubt Ryan had just finished a similar kind of shower.

"So, talk."

He took a swig of his beer as he waited.

"Do you think you can refrain from claiming her if we let her touch us? Damn, but I've been hard and aching all bloody day. The shower I just took barely helped. And honestly, I don't think Lacey is going to let us get away with keeping our pants on two nights in a row."

Dylan shrugged. "Well, if she doesn't like it, she can always agree to mate with us and then she'll get us both in all our naked, horny glory any time she wants."

The solution was simple, although his dick didn't agree. His dick was totally on board with Ryan's plan of getting some loving as soon as possible.

His twin rolled his eyes. "Seriously? You can't wait at all? She's allowed to take a few days to think about it. She wasn't raised in shifter culture, so she doesn't trust the strong connection she feels for us yet."

Dylan downed the last of his beer, the cold hops barely taking the edge off the raging inferno in his gut. "Let's just see how things go. If she wants to play with us, Ry, I doubt I'll be able to say no. But I'm not offering. I'll be able to hold myself back from biting her, but it won't be easy, and I refuse to volunteer for that kind of hell."

Ryan smirked, raised an eyebrow, and glanced at Dylan's groin. "As opposed to the kind of hell you're currently in?"

"Shut up."

With that, Dylan spun and left the kitchen. Ryan knew him too damn well to bother trying to win an argument with him. So, he headed straight for his bathroom, stripping as he went. He couldn't wait to get under the warm spray and let his thoughts wander with memories of Lacey writhing under their touch.

He flipped the tap on and waited for the water to warm, his mind already pondering what he could do to Lacey once he got his hands on her again. With his mind filled with images of her writhing body, he stepped beneath the spray and slid his palm over his water-slicked erection, groaning at the friction and the erotic images of Lacey that were flicking through his mind.

Half an hour and a couple of orgasms later, he ran a comb through his rapidly drying hair and headed back to the kitchen, where he found Ryan dressed and ready to go.

Dylan asked his brother, "So, any ideas on where we're taking our little mate tonight?"

"Well, if your gourmet tastes can handle it, I wondered about heading down to St. Kilda with her, grabbing some fish and chips and eating it down at the beach."

Dylan shook his head. "Yeah, that's a great idea and all, but Monday is the day all those places are closed. Also, she admitted to me on our date she doesn't like fish. Try again, little brother."

Ryan snatched up the keys with a growl. "You think of something, then."

"How about we drop into the pub to eat, then come back here?"

That way none of them would have to cook or do dishes, and they could get her back to the privacy of their house where they could enjoy their dessert—their sweet little mate's body.

Wiping his mouth on a napkin before he tossed it on his plate, Ryan turned toward Lacey. She was putting her fork down after taking her final bite.

"I picked the right booth, yeah?"

Lacey shook her head at him. "I'd wondered if you'd chosen it on purpose."

Dylan snorted. "Back to where it all began."

An adorable pink blush spread over Lacey's cheeks as she squirmed in her seat. "I'm a little ashamed at how I hid here spying on you both over the side of the booth."

"I thought you were cute. Well, once we worked out where you were hiding, I did."

Dylan nodded at him. "Damn air-conditioning spread your scent all over the place, so we had no fucking idea where you were sitting."

Lacey's hands went up in the air and her eyes widened. "Wait a second. You knew I was your mate from smelling me?"

Ryan winced, remembering that full humans didn't have the sense of smell shifters did.

Pushing his empty plate aside, Ryan held Lacey's gaze as he picked up one of her hands, savoring the feel of her soft skin on his fingers. He brought her hand up and ran the tip of his nose up her inner wrist, then pressed a kiss over her pulse point.

Was it his imagination or was her heart beating a little harder than it had a moment ago?

"Sweetheart, we both knew the moment this delicious scent of yours entered our noses that you were our mate."

"Well, well. Look who's crawled out from under their rock once again. Should have guessed you'd deal with the reporter by getting into her knickers. I suppose you'll both expect me to thank you or some shit for killing that story. Even if it was your skins on the line, not mine."

A frisson of rage tingled down his spine, and Ryan slowly turned to glare at Luke. As was typical, Dylan got in first.

"Shut the fuck up, that's our mate you're insulting, you asshole."

Ryan braced his feet to rise so he could follow up Dylan's first move, but Lacey derailed the natural order of how they dealt with issues.

"Leave it, Dylan. He's not worth causing trouble over."

Lacey's hand was on Dylan's shoulder holding him in place. The expression on his face said it all. He wanted to set Luke straight, but not at the cost of breaking their mate's contract with him. That was fine, Ryan was more than capable of stepping up and setting the stupid lion straight. Ryan was known as the level-headed one, the one that calmed everyone down ... but that was before he had a mate to protect, which included her honor.

He was done with being the reasonable one.

A vicious growl rolled through his chest and exploded from his throat. Ryan jumped up and pounced from his seat. He launched forward and plowed straight into a rather shocked looking Luke. The second they hit the floor, Ryan pulled back and landed his fist right in the bastard's face. He heard the crunch as pain flared up his arm, but he ignored both and bared his teeth.

"No one disrespects what's ours, especially not a cowardly fucking lion."

Luke held his palms up, eyes wide and blood pouring from his no doubt broken nose. Yeah, even a lion as stupid as Luke knew you never got between a cheetah and his mate.

"Calm the fuck down, dude. I'm sorry, okay? I didn't know she was your mate."

He continued to babble, and Ryan curled his lip in disgust. Bastard wasn't even man enough to attempt to get out from under Ryan, he just lay there and begged. What a wuss. No cheetah shifter would ever take a beating lying down, no matter what started it.

"Ryan! Ryan! Get off him right now. Oh my gosh! He's bleeding! What did you do to him?"

Dylan's firm grip on his shoulders pulled him up to face a near hysterical Lacey. Shit. He'd forgotten how most humans responded to violence.

Holding his breath for a moment, he silently begged, "Please let me not have just ruined our chance for a life with our mate."

A quick glance around showed that, fortunately, they hadn't drawn too much attention. Monday evenings were quiet as a rule, and tonight was no exception. And because the fight hadn't lasted more than a few minutes, they'd only gained a few raised eyebrows now that it was all over.

He looked back down at the lion and growled when Lacey kneeled beside him, holding a wad of napkins to Luke's nose while she held the back of his head.

"Ryan, deep breath. I know she's touching him, but it's only for medical reasons, okay? I really don't want to be kicked out of here for good. Trent said if we kept fighting with Luke, that's what'll happen. C'mon, bro. Deep breath."

His heart was pounding like a drum, and he couldn't seem to get his fists to uncurl. He still couldn't believe what Luke had said about Lacey. And he definitely couldn't believe Dylan was talking him down when it had always been the other way around.

The shock of Dylan making sense had him calming down enough to finally think clearly. He took a deep breath and reached out his hand to his mate.

"Leave him, Lacey. He'll be fine. I think it's time we headed out."

Lacey's belly twisted and churned. Her blood, heated with her fury, flooding her cheeks. She opened her mouth to bite something out at Ryan but instead her eyes were drawn to a waving Dylan behind his brother. He gave her a theatrical breathing sign and waved his hands towards the door, which had her frowning. Since when was Dylan the sensible one? While she hadn't known the twins long, she'd picked up quickly that Ryan was the cool, calm one while Dylan ran hot and fiery.

She let out her breath in a big rush, putting her hand in Ryan's. "Okay."

He pulled her up, and she glanced back at the guy on the ground. He was now being helped up by another guy, who looked like he knew the downed man. Where had he been when Luke had needed him before? She couldn't imagine Dylan leaving Ryan lying on the ground while another man punched him in the face.

She snorted out a laugh.

Not bloody likely.

Their loyalty to each other, their kinship and close friendship were some of the things she loved about them.

"Sorry about that, beautiful, but I wasn't letting him get away with talking about you like that." Ryan led her to the car, and they all climbed in, her in the back with Ryan, while Dylan took the driver's seat.

Ryan rested his hand on her thigh, and she flinched a little at the sight of his bloodied knuckles.

Ryan pulled his hand back. "Sorry."

"It's okay." She said the words, but her arms crossed over her chest, and she knew she'd lied. She didn't like violence, even petty stuff like that.

"I didn't like what he said about you, Lacey."

That wasn't a very good excuse. "Clearly. But, Ryan, here's the thing. He doesn't even know me, so his words don't mean a damn thing. It's nothing but hot air. And like hot air, it's easily ignored."

He leaned back in his seat, a grimace rippling over his handsome face. "But Luke does know us, sweetheart. Actually, he knows us both rather well. He was deliberately trying to hurt us by saying shit about you, and I wasn't standing for it."

Her hands fell into her lap, and she took a slow, deep breath. He was right. What that Luke guy had said was pretty nasty. And Ryan had only punched him the one time. Compared to what could have happened, it was pretty mild, really. If she was going to give this thing with the twins a serious shot, she needed to loosen her stance on violence. They were hot-headed men, with—literally—inner animals. Fights were bound to happen every now and then.

"I don't like violence, even basic brawls like that."

Dylan laughed from the front seat. "Sweetheart, I've never seen my brother throw a punch in my entire life. Be proud that he cares about you more than his pristine reputation for loving peace."

She gasped and looked back at Ryan, who was looking out the window. "Is that true?"

He shrugged and looked back at her with a smile. "I'm sorry you were upset, Lacey, but out here and in my family, we fight for our own. I've never felt the need to defend anyone before, but you're very different. I'll lay my life on the line for you any day, especially against a stupid, cowardly lion."

A pleasurable blush stole up her face in a hot wave. That was heavy. Her own mother barely wanted to see her, and here was a man willing to do anything for her. That was a bit beyond her comprehension.

She pulled her mind away from the implications of his words, latching on to the new piece of information.

"Lions? You've called him that twice now. What are they? Don't tell me there's more breeds of shifters out here beside cheetahs?"

Dylan huffed from the front seat. "Don't put them in the same box as us, please."

She rolled her eyes and looked back at Ryan. He'd explain things properly to her, without the sarcasm Dylan would lace the conversation with.

"Ryan?" She slid her hand onto Ryan's, careful to avoid the blood, and he turned his hand over, palm up, and their fingers intertwined. Pleasure shot through her veins, and she shivered.

"The lions are another family of shifters that live in this area. Our families have been feuding for generations."

"How come?" There had to be a reason for that.

"No one really knows, and to be honest, a few of them aren't too bad. But lions are very different from us. They're solitary creatures, unlike cheetahs, who are pack animals. The lions were the ones who tried to stop us finding Cameron and helping him. They like to plan, and very slowly deliberate every risk before taking one step forward. Naturally, we ignored them and helped young Cameron out. We knew that storm wasn't going to allow for all their rules to be followed if he was going to be rescued in time."

She laughed, the heat in the car now starting to work its way into her lower abdomen. "And don't forget, the added bonus of risking exposing shifters to the world at large by doing so."

Ryan had the decency to look a little bashful. "Yeah, well. Sometimes we have more heart than brains. So, sue us."

She leaned forward and kissed his lips gently. They were one block from her house, and she couldn't wait to take her men inside.

"I'll take heart over anything, any day."

Ryan and Dylan had telepathically discussed a change in plans after leaving the pub. Lacey was fired up about the fight, and Ryan hoped with the longer drive back to her place, she'd calm down and give him a chance to make amends.

His plan worked. By the time they'd pulled up to the front of her house, she was holding his hand and poking fun at them, the fight all but forgotten. Now Ryan sat on her couch, with his mate between him and his twin, as it should be. It always felt so right when Lacey was between them. What he really wanted was to have her naked between them.

"You're certain your roommate isn't going to come home any time soon?"

Lacey shook her head as she focused on undoing Ryan's shirt buttons. Seemed like she wanted him naked, too. He was so on board with that plan. Not wanting to stop her from what she was doing, he traced his fingers lightly over her thigh. A tease with no demand. Yet.

"I'm sure. She's working the late shift, so won't be home until after midnight and she knows you're both here, so she'll probably come in the back door to avoid potentially seeing us getting all hot and heavy."

Ryan let out a groan when she finally got his shirt open and began running her fingertips lightly over his chest and abs. Dylan moved her hair out of his way before he nuzzled his face in against her neck.

Lacey shuddered with a whimper before she shrugged away from Dylan's mouth.

"Not tonight. You're not going to distract me so easily. Last night you two got to play, so tonight is my turn. I want to touch and feel. Learn you both."

Ryan grinned at his feisty little mate and was sorely tempted to throw out a "told you so" at his twin.

"We're all yours, sweetheart, but don't expect either of us to sit here idly while you play. You need to get used to having four hands on you."

Dylan broke into the conversation with a whisper near her ear, "And two mouths. We're going to always want to be touching you or kissing you, beautiful."

She murmured a noise of agreement before she lowered her head and began kissing his chest. Ryan threw his head back as his body shuddered with his intense need of his mate. Her lips were branding him as she slowly nibbled her way over his muscles, and it was a memory he would never forget. This very first time his mate was touching him with love like this would be seared into his memory forever.

He held himself still as long as he could, to let her play, but soon he started shaking from the effort and knew he was done. Driving his fingers into her hair, he tugged her away from where she was laving his nipple and pulled her up so he could take her mouth with every ounce of passion he had in him.

She tasted like heaven. He held her head still as he dominated her mouth with his. She moaned and whimpered under the onslaught, but he didn't stop. He'd never stop needing this woman.

He felt her body move, and he opened his eyes to see Dylan taking her shoes off. Great idea. They needed their mate naked. Ryan ended their kiss and gripping her waist, stood with her in front of him. A pang of guilt hit him when she gasped, and her eyes went wide with shock.

"Sorry, babe. I didn't mean to scare you."

"It's just you're so much easier to strip standing up," Dylan finished his sentence as Ryan gave Lacey another kiss. When her body relaxed, he backed off and took hold of the bottom of her shirt. Making sure his fingers stayed in contact with her soft skin, he slid the garment off over her head. Dylan unclipped her bra, and Ryan licked his lips as he slid it off down her arms. Her breasts were perfect. They were large and soft and were tipped with the most responsive nipples he'd had ever tasted. Cupping one in his palm, he lifted it as he lowered his mouth until he could wrap his lips around the sweet nub. He grazed it with his teeth a moment before tugging and then sucking on it.

Lacey's short fingernails scraped over his scalp a moment before she gripped a handful of his hair while she sighed. With a low growl, he moved his mouth to her other breast while his hand kept kneading and plucking at the one he'd just suckled.

When she jerked and mumbled a curse, Ryan pulled away a little to see what Dylan was up to. Yep, his twin had his hand between her thighs and his mouth wrapped around her shoulder.

"Don't you bite her, Dylan. She has to agree to be ours first."

"Settle down, I'm not claiming her. My cat wants her marked, so we're compromising with some small love bites."

Ryan ran his gaze over her lush breasts, noticing he'd left a number of marks of his own, and his cat purred with contentment. She should always bear both their marks.

"Hmm, I was meant to be the one exploring you both, not the other way around. You already got your turn last night."

"Babe, we will never stop exploring this delectable body."

She actually growled a little at him while tugging on his hair.

"Can you both at least take your clothes off? It feels weird to be the only one naked."

Ryan took a deep breath and made sure his cat wasn't too close to the surface. This would be the biggest test. Having his naked, erect dick near Lacey's aroused, bare body was beyond tempting. And he knew if he made love to her, he'd claim her regardless of the fact she hadn't agreed to it.

That wasn't how he wanted to start their future together.

"Okay, sweetheart. You want us naked, you got it. But if we pull away suddenly, don't push us. We don't want to claim you until you agree to it, but we've only got so much willpower when we're with you—"

Dylan once more proved he was thinking the same thing as Ryan when he cut him off and continued the conversation seamlessly, "So instead of taking you before you say yes, we'll remove ourselves from the situation. But it's not because we don't want you or are rejecting you in any way. It's because we want you so much."

Lacey nodded and gave him a big smile. "Fair enough. Now strip. Neither of you gets to touch me again until both of you are completely naked."

She pressed her legs tightly together and folded her arms over her breasts, pushing the lush mounds up and making Ryan's mouth water. Lacey had already undone his buttons, so he had his shirt off in seconds before he tore into the fly of his jeans and toed off his shoes. All up, he only left her untouched maybe two minutes as he stripped and when he moved back to her, Dylan was buck-assed naked and pressed against her back already.

Chapter Fourteen

Lacey's whole body was aflame with need for her men once again. Dylan's hot, naked torso was pressed against her back while his rather large erection rested between her butt cheeks. She wriggled her hips to rub against his hot flesh and preened when he groaned and shuddered. Ryan stalking forward caught her gaze. His entire beautiful body was on full display in front of her. She had to find some control or tonight would turn out just like last night.

Not that she was complaining about how wonderful last night had been, but when she'd woken up this morning, she promised herself that tonight she would give back to the men who had so generously given to her.

She lifted both her hands and placed them on Ryan's pecs, her hands looking so small on the broad expanse of his chest.

"You're so..." She couldn't think of any word that fit, other than beautiful. It seemed odd to label a man like that, but it described him perfectly. Ryan's body was ripped, heavily muscled and strong. "Amazing."

He chuckled and stayed still as she toyed with his tiny pink nipples, then let her hands wander down the length of his torso. So flat, so muscled, so unlike her own body.

Dylan was kissing her neck and stroking her breasts. She tried to keep her concentration on Ryan, but she couldn't.

"Dylan, I don't suppose you could come stand in front of me too?"

Dylan stilled for a moment before he moved around her until he was standing beside Ryan, his body identical in strength and beauty to his twin.

"Wow." She let her gaze wander the length and breadth of both men. So much beauty, so much sexiness, so much male strength in one room. "How did I ever get so lucky?"

Dylan growled low, the sexy rumble coming out of his throat in a way that had her body coming alive without him even saying a word. He grabbed her hand and drew it down to his cock, the flesh already hard and thick and standing at attention in front of him.

In her rush to get ready earlier, she'd left out some moisturizer. Releasing her hold on him, she moved away to grab it. She used the lotion to lubricate both of her hands before returning to stand close enough that she could reach each of them.

"I can't wait to please you both the way you did me last night."

She closed her fists around both Dylan's and Ryan's cocks, and her men stepped closer, the heat of their bodies radiating out to her. They reached out and put their hands on her, their intense faces and roaming hands making arousal flood through her like a tidal wave. She stroked them both, up and down, glorying in their responses. They gasped and groaned, threw their heads back and growled. She pumped them harder, feeling their hands tighten on her in response, Ryan kissing her as Dylan slid his fingers between her legs again.

She opened to him, already hot and wet from the earlier attention, moaning as the ache inside her increased with the pressure of his fingers. Their abs buckled and rolled as she explored their flesh. The large, almost purple heads, the engorged veins flowing along their strong lengths.

Ryan tweaked her nipples with his fingers, and she groaned, arousal spreading through her body like wildfire. They strained against each other, racing toward their orgasms.

Dylan was the first to go over, groaning as he sank his fingers deep inside her while his cock jerked and spasmed in her hands. Ropes of his cum hit her hip and belly in hot bursts. Ryan was next, with his head thrown back he came, coating the other side of her torso with his seed, marking her.

Dylan moved forward and kissed her deeply, renewing his assault on her body, thrusting his fingers into her over and over until she, too, came with sharp, shuddering convulsions. As she came down from her high, she slumped forward. The men both leaned into her, holding her up as she tried to convince her legs to hold her weight.

"I think we could all use a shower," Dylan murmured against her lips, withdrawing his fingers from her body.

Lacey was ready to sleep for week. Her legs shook, she struggled to lift her arms, and her eyelids wanted to slide closed and stay that way. But she was coated in their seed and knew she wouldn't sleep well unless she got cleaned up. "I agree. Come with me."

Ryan chuckled. "Already did that, babe."

Chuckling at Ryan's remark, she led the men to the bathroom, turning on the shower. Once she'd adjusted the temperature, she slid beneath the hot spray, bringing them both with her. Grabbing her washcloth, she soaped it up then proceeded to wash their bodies, taking her time to enjoy their bulging biceps, rippling abs, and broad shoulders.

When the water began to cool, she turned the shower off. Once they'd all dried off, she led them into her bedroom, where they all climbed into bed. Lacey settled naturally into the center of the mattress, and her men curled around either side of her. She'd never felt as content as she did in that moment, and quickly fell asleep with Dylan's heart beating against her ear and Ryan's hand possessively curled around her breast.

On Friday, it was time to finish her newspaper article, and she was back at the zoo. She hadn't seen Dylan or Ryan for a few days due to their work schedules not lining up, but she was excited to be seeing them again tonight.

She turned to her best friend and gave her a smile in thanks.

"Laura, you really didn't need to come with me."

Laura huffed and rolled her eyes, and Lacey looked back at the road with a smile on her face. "But I do appreciate it."

"Yeah, well, I still don't trust that stalker ex of yours, plus I haven't been to the open range zoo since I was a kid."

Lacey grinned and took the exit off the freeway to the twin's work. She'd finished the article for the paper and wanted a photo of the cheetahs to finish it off.

After two days of pondering the merits of being true to Cameron's story and the need to hide the identity of the cheetahs, she'd decided to tell the truth. Most of it, anyway. Who was going to believe her anyway? She recalled the entire story with embellished flare, minus the names of her men, adding at the end of the story, "I didn't want to believe him, but after careful consideration I have stayed true to the report. After all, who am I to argue with the word of a four-year-old?"

If she was lucky, it would be great promotion for the zoo, too. More people coming to visit the zoo was always good, right?

"Here we are."

She pulled into the parking lot, a happy sigh bubbling up from inside her.

It was Friday, and tonight was another night with Ryan and Dylan. She'd spent the last few days thinking about how she was going to deal with her dilemma of what to do about her future. She had two men who wanted to mate with her, and although it felt so incredibly natural and beautiful to her, a ménage a trois in her world was not normal. How would everyone in her life react? Her friends, her family? Although, she wasn't particularly close with her parents, so even if they reacted poorly, it wouldn't be a huge issue.

In the end, she'd gotten herself so worked up and confused about it all that Laura had sat her down and yelled at her. Her best friend had brought it all down to one core point—you only live once, and who gives a fuck what other people think, so long as you're happy and not hurting anyone.

Now she was confident with her decision, happy to have the support of her best friend as she stepped outside of her comfort zone. She'd also already meet Ryan and Dylan's immediate family, all of whom seemed supportive of their relationship. And she'd liked them all, liked the family dynamic they shared. Even the teasing between the brothers was something she one day hoped her own children would share. She knew where the twins worked and that they had good, responsible jobs—a major plus. And lastly, she'd first given herself to these men expecting to receive very little in return, but that's not how it played out. Every time they were together, they had shown her tenderness, care, and the greatest pleasure she'd ever known.

She also trusted them, which was incredible in itself. After everything she'd gone through with her horrible ex, she'd been torn between the need of hiding away to keep herself safe from further hurt and her need to be wanted, to be loved and to love. Ryan and Dylan were tempting her to give them everything she had. To believe in the fairytale they were spinning around her.

"Let's go."

Laura grabbed her expensive camera and zoom lens, and they headed off towards the entrance.

"Are Dylan or Ryan here today?"

A smile lifted Lacey's lips. "I'm not a hundred percent sure, but I think so."

She hadn't messaged them to ask, not wanting to disturb them at work, but now that she was here, she was calling herself three types of a fool for not letting them know. They probably would have organized to be available for her.

"I should have called them."

Laura rolled her eyes. "Yes, you should have."

"Well, I didn't want to appear too needy."

Laura laughed. "From what you've told me, those boys want you so badly they'd drive to Perth and back just for a cuddle. Gotta say, I'm a little envious."

Lacey glanced away and stepped forward, paying for her and Laura's entrance while heat bloomed in her cheeks.

Monday night had been so incredible. She'd been horrified the following day when she'd realized she hadn't given anything to the men in return, but they'd both sent her beautiful messages about how much they'd gotten out of being able to witness her passion and moans.

Tuesday night had been even better. Being able to touch them, explore and pleasure them while they still gave so much to her, had been life changing. In the past, she'd only dared to dream men like them existed. She certainly hadn't thought she'd ever be lucky enough to get find one for herself. She'd squirmed all week from their messages and phone calls.

Tonight was going to be explosive.

"Which way are the cheetahs, Lace?"

"This way. We may as well start at the feeding pen where we can get a close-up, and then go see the ones on the safari bus."

They heard the rumble of the spotted cats before they rounded the corner to the front of the enclosure where they could see them, and a smile rose on Lacey's lips.

There they were. The incredible animals her men could turn into.

A chuckle broke free. Her men. She so liked the sound of that.

"What's so funny?"

She grinned at her friend. "Just thinking about Cameron's story. How cool would it be to have one of those rescue you from the side of a cliff?" She tilted her head towards the pen.

Laura shuddered. "Yeah, I don't think so. I probably pass out and fall off the damn cliff before they could reach me. Can't cheetahs rip your throat out if they want to?"

Lacey grinned at her rough and tumble, pistol-shooting blonde friend who was apparently scared of cats. "If they wanted to, I'm sure they could."

Since when was Laura scared of anything?

They stepped up to the viewing platform that was raised above the cheetah feeding yard.

Lacey looked down on the three cheetahs in the small pen. Two were lying in the sun, clearly relaxed, but one was pacing up and down the back fence in obvious agitation.

"Max."

She remembered his markings so knew it was him. A part of her ached to see him frustratingly stalking back and forth over the bare dirt. It was partly her fault he was stuck in this small yard, unable to shift back to human.

She swallowed hard against the uncomfortable ache in her gut, yet a smile twisted her lips. It wasn't all her fault that he'd been punished that night. The stunt he'd pulled on her hadn't been the kindest way to reveal to her the family's secret.

"Did you just call one of the cheetahs Max?"

She grinned at Laura. "Well, yeah. It is his name."

Laura raised an eyebrow her way. "You've been dating these guys for a week, and you already have pet names for the animals at their zoo?"

"No. That's their ... ah..." She cut herself off with a nervous laugh just in time. "Ryan looks after the cheetahs, so I know more about them, that's all."

Laura rolled her eyes and strode up to the balustrade, staring down at Max, who had now stopped moving and instead was gazing up at them. Lacey frowned. He wasn't staring at them both at all, but was solely focused on her friend. How strange.

Laura froze before she raised a shaking hand to point to where Max stood, head up alertly with his gaze still locked on Laura.

Laura cleared her throat before speaking, "Max is that one?"

"Yeah, why? What's wrong?"

"I ... don't know." Laura shook her head, but didn't move her gaze from Max.

Laura's behavior was so out of character, Lacey wasn't sure what to think. But they needed to get to work so they could get back home with enough time for Lacey to get ready for seeing her men tonight.

"Laura, are you going to take some photos?"

"Yes, yes!"

That got her moving. Laura reached for her camera, juggling the bulky item clumsily and almost dropping it as she pulled it roughly out of its case.

Lacey grabbed for the expensive zoom lens as it began to topple out of its black holder.

"Easy, Laura. Damn, what's up with you?"

When Laura began snapping photos, Max jerked out of his daze. The muscular feline began to prowl up and down the boundary fence like he was ready to attack. The hairs rose on Lacey's neck as Max rumbled and growled, his actions clearly showing he was one majorly pissed-off cat.

She didn't like it.

"Laura, I think we should go."

She tugged on Laura's elbow and her friend looked up from her frantic clicking.

"Are you sure? I can take some more pics."

She lowered her head to continue shooting, but Lacey pulled harder, not liking the strange behavior from either of them.

Max roared louder, and Lacey jogged away, dragging Laura with her.

"What was that?"

Laura shook herself and glanced back at the platform, a furrow between her eyebrows.

"I'm not sure ... but that cheetah was extremely beautiful, wasn't he? Perfect for an image to go with your article."

Completely spooked, Lacey didn't want to hang around anymore. Something was wrong with Max, and knowing he could turn human to get out of the enclosure if he choose to, had her wanting to get far away.

A park employee walked past, and she called out to him.

"Excuse me, but do you know if Ryan or Dylan Monaghan are working today?"

The older man smiled at her. "No, sorry. They've both got today off. I think they're both working tomorrow, though. Would have to check to be sure."

She smiled. "Thanks, no need to check. I'll give them a call later."

She pulled a still strangely immobile Laura back through the entrance and towards the car.

"Are you sure you're okay, Laura?"

"Yeah. Sorry. I uh ... think I've got plenty of photos good enough to go with your article."

Laura continued to scroll though the photos on her digital camera, clearly enthralled by all the images of Max she'd taken.

Lacey couldn't resist giving her a sarcastic response. "You think?"

With a shake of her head, she opened the car and slid in. Thankfully, Laura snapped out of whatever trance she'd been in, and got in the passenger seat, putting the camera away once she buckled her seat belt.

"You sure you're going to be all right tonight, Lace, when I go to work"""

Laura worked weekends, and Lacey often made plans to make sure she wasn't at home alone. But that wasn't going to be a problem tonight, or for the future either, she hoped.

Her belly tightened as warmth pooled between her legs. "Yeah, I'm sure. Dylan and Ryan are coming over tonight."

A low chuckle rose from Laura as she returned fully to her normal self. "Then I'll make sure I slip quietly in at four am and sleep 'til noon. Wouldn't want to disturb you."

Lacey smiled as Laura's laughter filled the car while they headed for home. Now she'd made her decision, she couldn't wait to tell the men. She was sure tonight was going to be a night to remember.

"Would you hurry the hell up? We could be halfway to Lacey's by now."

Refusing to react to Ryan's bitching, Dylan continued to carefully lift the container from the rear seat. As always, he enjoyed the sensation of how his palms warmed instantly from the heat soaking through from the food within the container.

Once he had the food safely out of the vehicle, he turned to glare at his brother. "I refuse to serve Max more fish coated in bloody dirt. The two minutes it takes me to be careful isn't going to slow us down by much. Especially since we're running over an hour early to begin with."

Dylan couldn't see any point in sitting outside Lacey's house waiting for her to get home from work, especially when they had other things to do. But his brother seemed to have other ideas.

Ryan rolled his eyes. "Lacey dropped the damn fish, not you."

He frowned over at his twin. "It doesn't matter who dropped it. It got ruined. I'm not going to put up with the shit I'll cop if Max runs to Mum at the end of his time to tell her I fed him mud-covered fish!"

Without waiting for any more commentary from his twin, Dylan headed up the path to find Max. When he reached the gate, his gut dropped, and he stilled. Something was wrong. So wrong it, tainted the air. Glancing around the yard, he saw Max pacing back and forth like a wild cat locked up for far too long. Every time his brother's cheetah paused, he'd growl at the fence with a menacing tone that bordered on dangerous. What the fuck was wrong with his older brother?

Ryan came up behind him and voiced his own concern at the strange behavior. "What's going on with Max?"

Moving forward past Dylan, Ryan opened the gate so they could both enter. No matter how agitated Max was, Dylan was confident he'd never attack his family. Not in a million years.

Dylan placed the container on the ground near the water trough and opened the lid, revealing a perfectly cooked trout, still warm and dirt free. He inhaled on a moan. The smell was delicious.

"Oi, Max! I got freshly baked fish for you!"

After a final snarl at the fence, Max prowled over to them and shoved his snout into the container where he inhaled the food as though he hadn't eaten for a week.

Dylan grinned as his brother enjoyed his cooking and elbowed his twin. "Guess he can't be too out of whack if he's still got his appetite, huh, bro?"

Ryan had deep frown lines across his forehead. "He wasn't like this yesterday. I wouldn't have thought he'd be feeling the pain from not shifting yet. It's only been a couple of days. Max? Talk to us. What's got you this worked up? Do I need to move you to the bigger yard?"

Max stayed silent until he finished eating every scrap of the fish, then he lifted his head and stared straight at them.

"I saw my mate."

"Holy shit! She came here? That's some crazy twist of fate."

Max rarely came to the zoo for more than a couple of hours to shift and go for a run. He was a builder and was always off in some rural town or farm working. The chances of him being here, especially in the feeding pen, when his mate came to the zoo were extremely low.

Ryan stepped closer to Max and got serious. "Do you know who she is?"

"She came with your mate earlier today. Her name's Laura."

Dylan started laughing. From what Lacey had told him, Laura was a very serious, tough, no-nonsense woman. Visions of her with Max, the comedian of the family, had him grateful that along with Ryan and Lacey, he'd get a front row seat to Max trying to win her over. This was going to be hilarious!

Max apparently didn't see the funny side because the bugger started growling.

"What's so fucking funny?"

"Laura is Lacey's roommate. Man, she plays at a pistol club for fun. Hell, she keeps her gun safe in their lounge room! Oh, watching the two of you work this out is going to be beyond entertaining."

Ryan thumped Dylan in the arm, hard enough that Dylan took the hint. Maybe he'd said enough, but his brother kind of deserved a mate who'd put him through the wringer and make him work for it. Laura would be perfect.

"Shut it, Dylan. Max, at least you know where she is and how to find her. I'll message Dad and ask him to come visit you so you can plead your case to get an early release. We'll ask Lacey a few questions for you, too. We're actually heading there when we leave here. She's never mentioned anything about Laura having a boyfriend—quit your growling—so I think you're in the clear on that score."

Dylan tried to hide his chuckle at Max's growling by leaning down to collect the now empty and licked clean container. Feeling cheeky, he reached over to ruffle the fur on Max's head, which earned him a snarl.

"You're too easy, Max. If you're still here in a couple of days, I'll bring you another fish." He turned to face his twin. "Hurry it up, Ryan, we've got our own mate to go catch."

CHAPTER FIFTEEN

After work, Lacey had stopped to grab a few things from the shops on her way home. The moment she exited her car, she sensed something wasn't right. A shiver coursed up her spine as she unlocked the front door and turned the lounge light on. She wasn't a superstitious person by nature, but when it came to trusting her instincts, it usually paid off when she followed them. Especially since her ex had started his bullshit.

She glanced around the room quickly before turning back to relock the solid wood door. Her heart banged against her ribs. Something felt strange, but nothing looked out of place.

"Stop it, you're being silly now."

Shaking her head at herself, she dropped her bag by the couch. Being stalked by her ex for so long had officially made her paranoid. She needed to focus on something more pleasant.

A smile rose to her lips as she thought about her day. Her new boss had loved her story on Cameron's rescue and the photos Laura had taken of Max. She really had to ask the boys about what had caused Max to behave like he had. Laura had certainly never acted as she had before.

She got a glass of water and when she glanced at the clock excitement bubbled up within her. It was not quite six o'clock. The twins would be there in an hour, then she'd have them both for the entire night. If she was brave enough to tell them she wanted to accept their claim on her, hopefully she'd have them for a lot longer than that.

A chuckle rose up her throat and she let it bubble out into a proper laugh. Her and two gorgeous men. Who would have ever thought?

She ran her palms over her slightly rounded belly and over her fleshy hips, a nervous habit she'd often done. Normally it caused feelings of shame and guilt to rise, but she didn't feel any of that today. Tears pricked her eyes when she realized that in just the short time she'd known the twins, their easy acceptance of her just as she was had enabled her to finally push aside the hang-ups she'd had about her weight for so long.

And it was more than just ignoring her size as many of her old boyfriends had done. They seemed to really want all of her—body and soul. She'd never known such levels of devotion even existed. It was a beautiful feeling to be cherished so deeply, and for the first time, she was looking into the future with hope for more of the same.

Lacey pushed open the door to her bedroom and stepped inside, her belly tightening with arousal as images of what was going to happen later tonight flashed across her mind.

The door shut behind her with a loud bang, and with a jump, she spun around as she pressed a palm over her heart. The hair on her nape prickled with a warning that was too late to save her.

"Hello, Lacey."

She jerked as his voice ricocheted around the room from where he stood leaning against the door, blocking her exit. The lazy smile on his lips made her skin crawl. It spoke of triumph and satisfaction. Two things she did not want him feeling while he was anywhere near her.

"Rodney. How did you get in here?"

And why the hell are you in my room?

"I'm smart. You know that. I'll always find a way to get to you, babe."

She nodded and backed away as he pushed off the door and took a few steps towards her. Where'd I leave my phone? By the front door! Fuck!

The backs of her legs hit the nightstand and she froze, assessing her options. Her heart started to pound in her chest and her mind raced. She wasn't getting on her bed if she could help it, but Rodney was a big guy. If it came to an actual physical encounter, she didn't think she would fare too well. But she sure as hell wasn't giving up without at least trying to fight him off.

Keep him talking. Hopefully the twins will come early, and they'll know be able to handle him.

With a deep breath, she set about placating him. "I know you're smart, Rodney, you always have been. But why'd you sneak in? Did you want to talk to me about something?"

Rodney stopped advancing on her and grabbed the chair by her dressing table, dragging it over to the door and jamming it up under the handle, effectively blocking her best exit. And stopping anyone being able to come in. There was the window, but he'd no doubt be able to grab her before could get it open and climb out. It wasn't worth risking making him angry by trying. At least not yet.

He chuckled, the sound low and menacing. "I've been trying to talk to you since you broke up with me, but you wouldn't respond." He shrugged a shoulder. "Now you can't get away so we're gonna have that talk."

She swallowed hard, bile rising from her churning stomach, but she pushed it down and ignored it. Dylan and Ryan would be here soon, in an hour at the most. Could she keep him talking for that long? She knew they'd protect her, even if it was just distracting him for long enough that she could get away.

"W-what do you want to talk about."

"Us, of course. I don't know why you turned against me, Lacey. I loved you, and you broke my heart."

Oh, please. There was only room for one love in Rodney's heart, and that was all for himself.

She kept her voice as calm and soft as she could manage. "I didn't mean to make you feel that way, Rodney. Honestly, I didn't."

"Then why break us up, Lacey?"

He sounded so reasonable she began to relax, her knees bending so that her butt sank towards the bed.

No. Don't let him get under your guard.

She straightened again. "I didn't think we were the right fit, Rodney. Our goals were so different and—"

"That's not true." His tone had darkened, the menace returning.

Lacey reached for something to say that would placate him. "You deserve so much better than me, Rodney. Someone with more brains, like you. I barely passed my course last year."

That was true, but it wasn't due to lack of brains. Stress and a lack of sleep had severely affected her ability to study.

She bit her lip hard as denial filled her whole mouth. He was an abusive asshole who she wished she'd never had the misfortune to have met, let alone shared a bed with.

Rodney reached into a black duffle bag she hadn't noticed he had at the end of her bed and pulled out a bundle of rope.

Oh, fuck no. Dylan! Ryan! Where are you? I need you! Please, please, please get here soon!

"Now, we're going to sit here all night if necessary and sort out our issues. I don't want to tie you up, but I will if I have to."

Laura's gun safe! It was in the next room and the keys were in her dressing table.

They weren't loaded, but he didn't know that. If she could just get to them, it may give her the advantage she needed to get Rodney out of her house.

"You don't need to tie me up, Rodney. I'll listen to you."

He stood up and looked at the floor, shaking his head like he was disappointed.

"No, I know you, and you'll run away when things get a little rough. You always do."

He stepped closer, and she dashed away from her bed.

"No, please don't, Rodney. You're scaring me."

"There's no need to be scared, Lacey. You can trust me, but I can't have you running off to be with those two zookeepers."

She swallowed hard, her hands quivering as she twisted away from him again and dove for the door, grabbing the chair and throwing it clear before reaching for the handle and pulling hard.

Rodney's hands came down, slamming shut the door and before spinning her so her back slammed against the door. He slapped her across the face with enough force that she stumbled to the side. Lost in shock, she was numb as he grabbed her again and shoved her hard toward the bed, where she had no choice but to fall onto the mattress.

The strike had caused fire to explode across her cheek. Her neck had cracked with the impact, and her head was still spinning.

His huge body was suddenly on top of hers, lifting her arms above her head and tying her wrists with the rope he held before she could think to react. Her brain was still settling from his harsh blow.

With his weight pinning her down, she struggled to take full breaths. Her heart pounded so loudly against her ribs, she was afraid it would burst through.

"Rodney, get off me!"

He lifted his leg and released the pressure, and she gasped out, sucking in air while she pulled her arms against the bonds, kicking her legs at him.

"Untie me now! How dare you! This is illegal!"

Terror fueled her struggles until white spots were forming at the edges of her vision as she got close to hyperventilating. She fought against her rising panic to breathe more steadily. The last thing she wanted was to pass out and put herself fully at his mercy.

She inhaled through her nose and breathed out through her mouth a couple of times before she lifted her head and glared at Rodney.

"You will regret this."

He chuckled while he returned the chair to sit in front of the door. But this time instead of shoving it under the door handle, he sat on it, making himself comfortable with the calm of a person who had all the time in the world.

"The only thing I regret is waiting so long to tell you how much you mean to me. But by the end of tonight, I'm sure you'll know."

Lacey shuddered and lay back, letting her arms relax as much as they could in their awkward position. She needed to save her strength for later. She had no idea what Rodney had in store for her, but she was damn sure she wasn't going to enjoy any of it.

Ryan's muscles were tense with anticipation. Each time they'd seen or spoken to Lacey during the week, she promised she'd make her decision by Friday. That was today, and Ryan had high hopes that she'd decided to accept them both as her mates.

"You don't think she'll try to choose only one of us, do you?"

Dylan's confidence when they'd left the zoo had evaporated, and now he sounded worried. While Ryan understood his twin's concern, but he was certain it was needless fear. Lacey was drawn to them both, had felt the mating heat the three of them shared.

"I think if we'd pushed her too hard in that first couple of days, she would have tried to take just one of us or neither of us. But after having those separate dates with us, she seemed to get that we're two halves of a whole. I'm certain she realizes we're a package deal at this point."

Dylan just grunted in response.

Ryan tried again, "Bro, seriously. If she was thinking like that, why was she kissing us both all week? Whenever one of us gets her all hot, she always stops to make sure we're both with her. Haven't you noticed? She knows that she needs both of us to be complete."

A rough laugh came from Ryan's twin. "I hadn't noticed. Whenever I was that close to her, I was completely distracted. Okay, so she's going to say yes to being our mate. Do you think she'll have packed her stuff up already?"

Ryan jerked in his seat. "What the hell are you on about?"

"Well, if she's our mate, she lives with us, yeah? I want to move her in tonight. We can load up her stuff onto the tray and take her back with us. That's why I brought the ute. Then we can claim her in the bed—in the home—we'll share for the rest of our lives. Do it properly."

Ryan shook his head on a laugh. His twin really was a caveman. "You're welcome to try, brother. But I doubt it will be that cut and dry. She works in the city, about to have her first big story published—remember? I'm not sure she's going to want to live out in the country right now."

Dylan's look of horror made him laugh. "That's bullshit. Of course, she'll want to be out there with us. Clean air, no traffic, surrounded by nature. What chick wouldn't want that?"

Ryan gave up on his clueless brother. Lacey would have to tell Dylan how she wanted it to work herself.

"Well, we're here now so maybe you should ask Lacey how she feels about moving, rather than simply planning it all out for her."

They opened their doors at the same time, and instantly Ryan knew something was wrong.

"Oh, for fuck's sake!"

Clearly, Dylan had picked up the same vibe.

"You can say that again." Ryan paused to take another deep breath, trying to get a better feel on what was up. A familiar smell hit his nose. "Her ex is here."

The bastard had to still be here for his scent to be so strong. Without another word, Ryan reached back into the vehicle to grab his go-bag. They each kept a bag in both of their vehicles with a change of clothes just in case they needed to shift in a hurry and ended up destroying what they were wearing. He slung the bag over his shoulder, and they moved silently away from the car, following the scent trail. When it led to a shattered window at the rear of the house, Ryan's fingers tightened into fists. He wanted nothing more than to keep following the trail inside to see exactly where he was. But he stopped, breathing deeply to calm himself.

"Why'd you stop? That bastard is inside! I can smell Lacey. He's in there with her."

"I know, Dylan, but think for a second. What if he has a gun on her or a knife? We go barging in he could seriously hurt her. Let's go back to the car and ring Eli. Tell him the situation and that we're going in. We need back-up here. Especially if she's hurt, Eli can get medical help on its way just in case."

"The only reason I'm not already through that busted window is because I can't hear her screaming."

Funny his brother felt that way, because it was the lack of noise that scared the fuck out of Ryan. What if they were too late?

"Fuck going back to the car, follow me."

He led his twin into the backyard and moved as far away as possible so they wouldn't be heard inside the house. He pulled his phone and rang Eli.

"Eli here."

"Hey, Eli. We're at Lacey's and can scent Rodney's in the house with her. We've got no idea how long he's had her, but we're going in to get her."

"Before you do, give me a recap of what you know."

"We arrived, scented him and knew it was fresh. We followed it to a broken window at the rear of the house. We can't hear any noise or voices from where we are, but we can smell Lacey's in there with him. We don't have time to wait for the police. It could already be too late."

He sighed through the line. "Yeah, I hear you. Do what you have to. I'm on my way."

"Thanks, and Eli? Best bring an ambulance with you, too. It really is way too quiet for my liking."

"Of course. Now go get your mate, stay alive, and try not to kill Rodney."

Ryan hung up without responding. There was no point in giving the man what he'd know was a fake promise.

"Okay. Let's go get our mate. Think we can make it through that broken window?"

Dylan jogged over to a pile of bricks against the side fence. Not wanting anyone inside to overhear them, he switched to telepathy.

"Seriously? Breaking another window isn't going to help."

"Keep your fur on. I'm getting her spare key."

"How do you know about her spare key?"

The arrogant cat just smirked at him before heading towards the back door. Ryan held his breath as Dylan carefully slid the key into the lock and twisted it. With a quiet snick, it opened and swung in. Ryan sent up a silent prayer that they weren't too late as he prowled down the hallway behind his twin.

CHAPTER SIXTEEN

Dylan had never experienced terror like this before. He could barely hear through the sound of his blood rushing in his ears, his palms were slick with sweat, and his imagination was coming up with all sorts of horrific scenarios. Please be alive. Anything else they could deal with. So long as Lacey was still here with them and breathing ... they would find a way to cope.

Following the sound of a low male rumble, he headed further into the house. A red haze clouded his vision when he realized the sound was coming from her bedroom. She was alone in there with her stalker. What had their mate already been forced to suffer through?

He stopped when he stood in front of the closed door. Squeezing his eyes shut, he focused on his hearing. With his shifter-hyper senses he should be able to work out roughly where in the room the bastard was, and whether it was safe to break down the door. He hadn't heard Lacey's voice at all yet, and his cat was pushing hard to get free to save their mate.

"See? We're good together. You just forgot how good it feels with me."

Pure rage washed over Dylan, and his body vibrated as his cat pushed harder than he ever had before, demanding to be set free. It took every ounce of willpower he had to keep himself in human form, because his cheetah couldn't open a damn door.

Ryan's presence behind him bolstered his confidence as he gripped the doorknob with a firm grip and holding his breath, he slowly twisted it. He opened the door just a fraction to test if there was anything blocking it and silently cursed when it hit resistance.

"There's something blocking the door. On three I'm going I shove the door in."

"Do it."

If it was something small, it would probably end up being tossed across the room. But they had one chance to make a surprise entrance, and he wasn't going to risk wasting time getting the bloody door open. He hoped he took out the guy and didn't hurt Lacey with the move.

"One, two, three."

Using every ounce of his shifter strength, he shoved the door open. With a terrible ripping sound, the door's hinges tore from the frame and along with a chair, the door crashed to the side of the doorway. Dylan didn't give it more than a micro-second of attention. His cheetah howled and took over, shredding his clothes as his strong feline form broke free of its human cage. He had no chance of holding the beast back now that he could see his mate. The sight of Lacey tied to the bed, gagged and half naked with some bastard on top of her would forever be seared into his mind.

"What the fuck?"

Rodney jumped off the bed with a high-pitched squeal of terror as Dylan leapt onto the mattress. He quickly, but carefully placed his paws so he stood over his mate, using his body to keep her protected beneath him. Without looking at his mate, he bared his fangs and snarled at the one who'd dare cause her pain.

While Rodney stood still, his eyes wide with shock, staring at Dylan's cheetah form, Ryan had slipped up behind him. In a couple of lightning-fast moves, Ryan had Rodney pinned to the floor with one arm twisted up behind his back. There was a crunch, and the man started blubbering, whining about being hurt. Dylan purred a little. He hoped Ryan just broke his shoulder or elbow. Preferably both.

Once sure that Ryan had Rodney under control, Dylan turned so he could look into his mate's eyes. Tears were streaming down her face, and her whole body shook violently beneath him. With a quiet whine, he lowered until his belly touched her bare skin. He gently licked at her tears before he carefully took hold of the gag with his teeth and tugged the material down out of her mouth. The moment her lips were free, she opened them wide to gulp in deep breaths of air. Dylan raised himself slightly to allow her to take deeper breaths.

"Oh, shit. Dylan, my Dylan. You came for me. He hurt me, oh bloody hell. He was going to really hurt me, but you came. You saved me."

She started moaning and pulling on her arms. He looked up and saw her hands had been bound with rope to the headboard, and blood was trickling down her forearms from how hard she'd tried to pull free. Balancing his weight on three paws, he lifted the other to swipe at the rope with his powerful, sharp claws, being careful to not nick his mate. When the rope snapped, freeing her, Lacey winced and groaned in pain as she tried to lower her arms from above her head.

"Dylan, shift back. She needs you to be human. Push your cat down, brother. You need to massage her arms and hands to get her blood flowing again. And I can hear sirens. We don't want the police or medics seeing a cheetah outside the zoo. C'mon, brother."

He knew his brother was right, but his cheetah didn't want to let go. He wanted to be the one to care for their mate, to make sure she stayed protected. He forced his cheetah to truly look at Lacey, at the pain she was suffering because no one was able to help her. Unlike domestic cats, a cheetah's claws didn't fully retract, so even if his cheetah wanted to, he couldn't even attempt to massage her. He'd tear her up.

That realization seemed to get through to his cat, and he was able to leap from the bed and shift back to human.

"Come and grab my bag and get dressed first."

"Yeah, the first responders don't need to be getting a load of my junk."

As fast as he could and without giving Rodney even a glance, he dressed and returned to Lacey.

"Hey, beautiful."

"Dylan."

Her voice was rough, like she'd been trying to scream through the gag, and it tore at his heart. With his eyes squeezed shut, he leaned in and pressed a kiss to her forehead before he picked up one of her arms. After helping her lower the limb and almost crying himself at the look of intense pain in her eyes, he rubbed and massaged her biceps and forearms until she stopped whimpering. Then he repeated the process for the other side.

Her clothes were a mess. Her shirt had been ripped down the center, and her bra cups shoved down under her breasts, exposing her perfect flesh. It couldn't be comfortable, and with as much care as he could, he slipped his fingers inside the cups to allow each of her breasts to settle back inside the protection of the lacy material. Her pants had been torn open, but her panties seemed to be intact. Thank the Fates for that!

Considering Rodney's fly was undone, anything could have happened if they hadn't arrived when they did. Dylan's cheetah rose to the surface once again, wanting to be freed, but he pushed it down. Lacey needed her human mates at the moment, not her cheetahs.

Sirens now filled the air, and Dylan could see blue and red lights flash down the hallway. They must have pulled up onto the front lawn. He quickly folded each side of the blanket over Lacey so she was covered.

"I'm going to go let the police and medics in. I'll be right back."

She nodded but her eyes filled with tears. His heart ached for what she'd gone through, and he wanted nothing more than to bundle her up and take her home where they could keep her safe. But they needed to do this properly, so Rodney got taken care of for good.

With a wince, he reluctantly left the room to head towards the front door and the person who was currently pounding on it.

Ryan stayed where he was as Dylan left the room. He had Rodney pinned to the floor with his knee in the center of his back keeping him there. The brutal arm lock he had on him in didn't hurt either. Well, it did hurt. But only Rodney, so it was fine.

A whimper from the bed had him wincing. Ryan wanted nothing more than to go to her and comfort her, but until the police took Rodney into custody, he couldn't.

"Lacey, sweetheart, I'm still here with you."

She hadn't even looked at him since they came in. Was Dylan right? Did she only want one of them? What would he do if she rejected him and only accepted Dylan? Could he honestly stand aside so at least his twin would know happiness? He hoped he could be that big of a person. But it would break his heart every time he saw them, and he'd never get his own family. Never raise cubs of his own. It would gut him for sure.

His gaze was locked onto her, so when she stilled at the sound of his voice, a lump formed in his throat. Images of a life alone without his twin or mate beside him filled his mind. Internally his cheetah howled in agony, and his own mind swirled in a downward spiral of darkness.

Then she rolled onto her side, facing him. She winced when she saw Rodney, before she lifted her gaze to his. Ryan took a deep breath when her expression softened, and a small smile tugged at her lips.

"My precious Ryan."

Her eyes filled with tears, and she did nothing to stop them as they fell. Ryan's own vision went hazy with unshed tears. His mate wasn't rejecting him.

"Hey, sweetheart, don't you worry about a thing. Dylan and I have got this. We'll have you safe and sound tucked into bed at our place before you know it."

She nodded a little as she brought her knees up so she was in a fetal position. He wished the cops would hurry the hell up. He wanted to be holding her on the bed, not this asswipe on the floor.

"I know, Ryan. You and Dylan will always take care of me. I'm not sure what I did to deserve such wonderful men in my life..."

"They're not fucking men. They're nothing but mons—"

Ryan slammed Rodney's head hard and fast into the hard timber floorboards, cutting off anything else the bastard was going to say as he became preoccupied with the new flare of pain in his skull.

"You will never say a word of what we are. If you do, we will find you. Even in jail we will get to you. If you ever become tempted to out us, just think about the kind of mess two fully grown, pissed-off cheetahs would leave you in. It won't be pretty, or much fun. Not for you, anyway. If you even manage to survive it."

Rodney shuddered but thankfully stayed silent. Dylan led the police in, Eli in the lead.

"You can get off him, Ryan. I'll take him from here."

More than happy to hand over custody of Rodney to the lion, Ryan released his hold on the man and stood.

"I might have dislocated his shoulder, and he hit his head on the floor when I took him down."

Eli grabbed Rodney off the floor and roughly shoved him against a wall, holding him there as he called into his radio to get one of the medics to come check out the shoulder. Then he turned back to face me.

"Unfortunately, the law prevents me from ignoring such obvious injuries. But don't worry, I'll make he get the maximum penalty for what he pulled today and in the past."

He gave the lion a nod of gratitude, then watched as medics came in and Rodney was taken out. Dylan shadowed them to make sure the bastard actually ended up being taken in after the medics were done with him. Once the group were out of sight, Ryan turned to rush to where Lacey lay curled up. He kneeled down beside the bed and stroked her hair while she rolled over so the medics could begin checking her over. They made fast work of cleaning up and bandaging the wounds at her wrists as he watched over her.

While they physically checked to make sure she didn't have any other injuries that needed tending, they peppered her with questions. It was bloody hard to hear the details of how his mate had been injured, and he wanted nothing more than to go kill the bastard responsible.

"Were you raped?"

Fuck, that one question struck a knife to his soul.

"No, he..." She paused to lick her lips. "He was going to. He used his fingers, but my men interrupted him before he took it further."

Relief coursed through me at the confirmation we'd been in time to prevent him from forcing sex on her. When they'd finished asking questions and examining her, she turned to face him, her red-rimmed eyes filled with tears again. Cupping her face, he gently pressed his lips against hers just for a moment, before he wrapped her in his arms again while she returned to answering questions, this time from Eli and another officer.

Lacey woke when large, work-roughened hands slid over the skin on her feet, massaging her, then soft, masculine lips were against her neck, pressing kisses against her sensitive flesh.

"Hmmm, morning."

She stretched carefully between the two men who were surrounding her and blinked her eyes open slowly. Her shoulders ached from last night and she still had a slight headache, but all in all she felt physically good considering what she'd been through. Mentally was a completely different story, but she refused to look too deeply into that yet.

"Good morning, beautiful. We have breakfast for you if you're ready to eat?"

Delicious smells had her tummy rumbling, so she moved to sit against the headboard. The moment she was settled, a tray was slid across her lap filled with pancakes, fresh blueberries, and a glass of juice.

"I ... um, thank you."

Ryan, who had moved to sit near her feet, gave her a big grin. "No problem. Dylan did most of that, of course."

Lacey blinked away the tingling threat of tears and wrapped her fingers around the juice. Lifting the glass, she swallowed some of what had to be freshly squeezed orange juice. The cold liquid relieved her parched throat, and she moaned at how good the relief was.

These two men were so full of thoughtful gestures, they never seemed to stop.

"I didn't fully consider the advantages of Dylan being a chef."

"One of many perks, I assure you." Dylan winked, and she smiled at him as her heart warmed.

"I can imagine." Suddenly, her exhaustion overwhelmed her and all she wanted to do was lie back down and sleep. She eyed off the mountain of food in front of her. A full stomach would hopefully help give her some energy. She swallowed more of the sweet, tangy orange juice before she took a bite of blueberries and pancake. The pancakes were fluffy and light, but her shoulders were so stiff she struggled to move enough to eat.

"What's wrong, sweetheart? How can we make you feel better?"

She must have moaned out loud without realizing it. She hadn't wanted to reveal she was still hurting.

"I don't know."

Her muscles would loosen once she could get up and move around, but she was feeling so tired, she knew she'd land on her face if she tried to get out of bed at the moment, so there really wasn't anything they could do. Same with her mental state. She knew she couldn't push down her emotions for long, but she didn't want them to explode out of her while the men were here to witness it. Maybe she needed a little time alone to process everything. But did she really want them to go?

"Could you take this away for me? I'm suddenly not hungry."

Dylan squinted at her for a moment, like he was assessing her health with his gaze before he moved to take her breakfast tray away. Tears burned her eyes as Dylan and Ryan yet again made their care for her obvious with their actions. They tried so hard to always make sure she was comfortable and had everything she needed. It was so strange to be pampered like this after she'd had to take care of herself for so long.

"How are you feeling?" Ryan asked, moving up the bed to take her hand and squeeze it reassuringly.

She had to be honest, with both them and herself. She dropped her head so they couldn't see her eyes. "Lost. Alone."

Dylan growled a little, and her head snapped up. She hadn't meant to upset them. She knew she wasn't physically alone, but she was struggling to get her thoughts straight in order to explain to them.

"Sorry, I didn't mean it like that. It's just ... I don't really have any family and..." Her mother hadn't shown her any love or compassion when she'd called last night to say she'd been attacked and injured but would be okay, and it had been years since she'd heard from her father so after dealing with her mum, she hadn't even bothered trying to get hold of him.

"Yeah, you do. You have a whole big, rowdy family just waiting for you to let them into your life."

She frowned at him, waiting for him to explain how she'd magically gained this new family.

"Us, Lacey, us! We want to be your family. And we come with seven big brothers and a set of parents who will smother you in love for as long as you can handle their overbearing natures."

Tears coursed down her cheeks as warmth began to fill her chest, pushing out the ice that Rodney had wedged in there last night when he'd abused her body.

"You still want me? Despite ... everything?"

As soon as she said the words, she realized that was the true reason she'd felt so terrified this morning. She'd feared that once Ryan and Dylan saw the sort of men she used to date, men that would take her against her will and abuse her, they wouldn't want her anymore. She felt so dirty and used ... definitely not pure enough to deserve the two beautiful men before her.

Dylan exploded up from where he'd been sitting on the side of the mattress, throwing his hands up in the air. "Of course, we do! We love you! You're our sun, our moon, our everything. Nothing is ever going to change that. Especially not some fuckwit who thought he could just take you and do horrible things to you. Don't you get that? Last night was not in any way your fault."

She shook her head, the tears still flowing, her throat closed off to words. She'd assumed they'd blame her for the attack. She blamed herself for it. If only she hadn't dated him the first place, it wouldn't have happened.

Ryan took over from Dylan. "Just because you dated him in the past, did not give him permission to assault you, baby. This was not your fault. I need to hear you say it, to know you believe it."

She smiled through her tears, forcing out the words. "It was not my fault."

"What wasn't your fault?"

She turned to Dylan who stood like a warrior with his arms crossed over his broad chest as he'd spoken.

"It wasn't my fault that Rodney attacked me."

With a grunt he nodded, and Ryan moved to kneel in front of her. "Lacey, be ours. Please agree to mate with us. We vow to stay by your side forever if you'll allow us. We will both support you, love you, and one day—hopefully soon—we'll have children to raise together. Anything you want."

"You really..." She tried to force out a whole sentence, but the words wouldn't come.

Ryan's blue eyes bored into hers, clearly pleading with her to give them the answer she'd been ready to give them before her ex had ruined everything yesterday.

"Say yes, Lacey. Please say yes to us."

Dylan's desperate tone got her moving. She nodded. She couldn't do anything else. The words were trapped inside her closed throat. But she meant them with all her heart and soul.

"Yes? You mean it?"

The uncertain look on Ryan's face as he'd spoken cracked her heart open. She cleared her throat, then wet her lips.

"Of course, yes. I love you. Both of you. How do we ... uh, mate?"

They grinned and surged toward her, making her grin in happiness. Between the two of them, they carried her until she was lying on her back on the bed.

"We make love to you, both of us, at the same time."

CHAPTER SEVENTEEN

Lacey reached her hand up to cup Ryan's face. That sounded simpler than she'd imagined it would be. She'd had visions of animals and markings.

Dylan grabbed her other hand. "And there's the biting. Can't forget that part."

Lacey stiffened. "Biting?"

Ryan frowned over at Dylan. "You could have worded that better, bro. Way to scare our mate." He turned his focus back on her, his eyes serious. "To complete the bond, after we make love, we'll each mark you." He ran a finger down where her shoulder met her neck. "I'll place mine right here, and Dylan will place his on the other side. But don't worry about it, there's no pain. It's a shifter magic thing, not a real bite. And once it's done, all shifters will be able to see our marks on you and know who will rip them apart if they dare touch you. We won't allow anyone or anything to take you from us. Not ever."

To be loved forever—truly bonded—sounded incredible. So much more than a marriage, which was nothing more than a piece of paper that could be tossed aside as soon as one person wanted to. This would be real and forever.

"All right then, my answer is still yes. I don't ever want to be away from either of you."

Dylan swooped in for a kiss, crushing her lips against his. Lacey wound her fingers through his hair while her eyes slid closed and warm pleasure oozed through her center like honey.

Ryan's hands tugged at her clothes. She'd only put on one of his t-shirts before she'd climbed into bed last night. After the attack she didn't feel right naked.

Dylan pulled away from their kiss to help Ryan tug the t-shirt off over her head, leaving her completely bare to them both. Feeling a little vulnerable, she lowered her gaze, but Dylan was having none of that. He cupped her face in both palms and retook her mouth, kissing her until she melted against him. He only wore track pants, so her chest came up against his hot flesh. A shudder ran through her as his light dusting of chest hair brushed over her already hard nipples.

Slowly, he ended the kiss, sipping at her lips until he pulled back completely. She blinked open her eyes and stared into his piercing blue stare. The look in his eyes made her heart beat faster in recognition.

But of what?

Then one single thought filled her mind.

My mate.

Something new began to purr inside of her as she embraced the destiny before her. She had been born for these men. To love them, to live with them. She knew it as surely as she knew her own name. The need for her men was a fire burning inside of her now that she'd accepted their claim on her. Hungry, burning, and insatiable. Why had she waited so long to agree to be theirs?

"I love you. I can't wait to mate with you."

Dylan groaned and slid from the bed. Before she could get upset at him leaving her, noise drew her attention to Ryan, who had now stripped completely. She couldn't help but stare in wonder. He was gorgeous, his body strong, lithe and full of lean muscle. And his hard cock pointed straight at her like a compass needle pointing true north.

She lifted her arms and gestured for him to come to her, and didn't need to ask twice. Instantly he began crawling across the bed toward her with lust burning in his gaze.

He kept moving until she lay caged beneath him. When he lowered down, she spread her legs to give him room. He echoed her moan when their hot flesh touched, their skin purring in rapture of being together again. And this time there would be nothing stopping them from bonding as one. No way would she ever let her men get away with pleasuring her with no chance for her to reciprocate again.

Ryan kissed her, scattering her thoughts as his tongue began tangling with hers just as their bodies soon would. He kissed her nose, her cheeks, then moved down to her neck, nipping and biting at the tender skin there.

She arched her back as he moved down to her breasts, shifting to lie next to her. A whimper left her at the loss of his body heat, but a second later she felt Dylan's hands on her thighs as he parted them further to give himself room to lie between them.

"Oh my..."

Dylan set his tongue to her slit before he licked his way up to her clit, and she cried out, pulsing pleasure moving through her blood, heating her up from the inside out, along with the air around them.

The men worked on her together, completely in sync with each other as they pleasured her in ways she'd only ever read about. She couldn't believe that this was her current reality, and her future. Happy tears slid down her cheeks as sensation after hot sensation bombarded her nervous system.

"I'm so lucky."

Ryan lifted his head from her breasts and grinned at her. "We're all so bloody lucky that we found you while we're so young. It's basically unheard of that the youngest cubs of a family find their mate first."

"Quit your babbling, bro, and get back to working our girl over. We can talk mushy shit later."

Lacey's eyes rolled back when Dylan delivered another wicked stroke to her core with his extremely talented tongue. When she blinked her vision clear, Ryan had moved up to kneel beside her head. With a grin, he leaned over her, so the engorged head of his very fine cock was near her mouth, tempting her to lick and taste it.

She groaned as Dylan sank his tongue into her pussy again before she opened her watering mouth for Ryan. She couldn't wait to have his taste on her tongue.

The skin of his cock was hot, smooth, and sweet as it passed through her lips. She moaned as tingles began running through her body. Between Dylan's spectacular oral skills and the sweet taste of Ryan's arousal on her tongue, she had her hands clenched into the sheets beside her in an attempt to stay grounded.

She groaned louder, arching up as an orgasm tightened in her core, ready to blow.

Then Dylan was gone from between her legs, and she pulled off Ryan to growl her frustration. She was so close to coming! She wanted him back down there to finish what he'd started.

With a smirk, Dylan ignored her glare and noises of displeasure as he prowled up the mattress until he was kneeling on the other side of her head, offering her his cock for some attention.

"I need your mouth on me, beautiful, like you wouldn't believe."

Moving to face Dylan, she reached her hand to wrap her fingers around Ryan's length. She began stroking Ryan's cock as she took her first lick of the bulbous red head of Dylan's erection.

When Ryan gasped and pulled out of her grip, she focused solely on Dylan, using her lips and tongue to return the amazing pleasure he'd just given her. After a minute or so, he also pulled free of her, making her whimper at the loss.

"Get up on top of Ryan, gorgeous. It's time."

Pleasuring them both at the same time had kept her arousal simmering just below climax, it was so bloody hot. Now, with the promise of fulfillment being so close, she rushed to slide her body over Ryan's. Her skin was hypersensitive, and as she rubbed over his hard, muscular frame, she purred like a kitten.

She slid up until she could press her lips to his. A sigh escaped her when he took over control of the kiss and thrust his tongue into her mouth to tangle with hers. Strong hands gripped her hips and moved her until she could feel Ryan's hot length pressed against her lower belly. She wriggled until his cock slipped between her thighs so his smooth head was pressed against her wet entrance.

"Oh, yesss."

Placing a palm against each pec, she pushed herself upright as she thrust back, lowering herself down his shaft. She was desperate for him to ease the deep ache she had inside her.

"Oh, fuck..." Ryan moaned beneath her as she swiveled her hips over him.

He grabbed her hips with rough hands and stared up at her, fire in his blue eyes, his mouth open as he panted for breath.

"Lie down against me, sweetheart. Give Dylan some room to play."

Dylan's large, warm palm pressed down on her back, between her shoulder blades, and she followed his cue. She leaned forward, kissing Ryan as her breasts flattened against his chest.

Dylan's fingers tapped on her back hole, and she flinched.

"What are you—"

"This is how we're going to take you together, sweetheart. Don't worry, you're made to take both of us."

She doubted that very much but pushed the negative thoughts aside. Although she'd thought they'd meant she'd have one in her mouth and one in her pussy, the thought of taking Dylan her ass had more heat flowing through her veins.

These men had never hurt her, or even disappointed her. They certainly hadn't ever lied to her, so she chose to trust them now.

"All right."

Dylan leaned over to open the drawer on the bedside cupboard, grabbing out a bottle of lube. Heat flashed over her cheeks and to distract herself, she turned her attention back to Ryan, who was gently thrusting inside her, and kissed him. Dylan's fingers probed and spread lube, the pressure tolerable, but strange. He pressed into her with his fingers, scissoring and stretching her. A moan rolled up her throat, and Ryan lifted her a little higher so he could increase his thrusts.

Sparks started to filter through her brain, the pleasure from Ryan's cock in her pussy and Dylan's fingers weaving together and building the pleasure higher with each stroke.

Oh, my.

Dylan's fingers disappeared and she missed them instantly, an unfamiliar ache deep in her body.

Then he was close behind her, his hands taking the place of Ryan's on her hips as he pressed his hot cockhead to her virgin entrance.

She held her breath and pushed back, burrowing her head against Ryan's chest as he continued his measured gentle thrusts. She inhaled, Ryan's sweet scent calming her as Dylan moved deeper within her.

Heat and pain pierced her as Dylan stretched her. She let out a gasp, and he forged forward with tiny thrusts of his hips until they were all melded together.

There was pain, but it was fading, leaving behind a sense of intensity.

"Oh, damn. I feel so full. Impossibly ... full."

"You're so bloody beautiful. So amazingly tight," Dylan panted in her ear, grabbing tightly to her hips as he started to move, and Ryan countered his twin's movements with increasingly powerful thrusts.

She gasped and sucked on the skin covering Ryan's collarbone, her fingers wrapping around his biceps, seeking an anchor in the tumultuous storm.

They seesawed back and forth, working a perfect tempo, all three of them heaving and gasping, chasing their completions together. Ryan started to keen beneath her, and Lacey tilted her pelvis just a little higher, searching for the perfect connection among all three of them.

He cried out as he came inside her, his cock pulsing into her womb, setting off her own orgasm. Her body exploded with sensation, and she cried out as the pleasure rolled over her in a huge wave.

Dylan moaned above her, thrusting into her one last time before filling her ass with his hot cum. Her body gathered itself and squeezed tightly again, milking both cocks still within her, loving everything they did to her.

Dylan wrapped her hair around a hand as he tugged her head back, revealing her throat to Ryan. Just as she began to tense up at what was to come, they both struck at the same moment, sharp teeth sinking into each side of her throat. As Ryan had told her, the sensation wasn't pain at all, but pleasure more intense than she'd ever felt before. Another orgasm barreled through her, and she screamed as her whole world shattered and fell apart.

She regained awareness as Dylan withdrew, leaving her wincing at the tenderness of her body as he fell to the bed beside her. A moment later, Ryan rolled them to the side and slipped free of her body then Dylan's arm wrapped around her and pulled her back against him as bliss continued to swim through her brain. She couldn't lift her arms or open her eyes.

She tried to speak. Opened her mouth to say something, yet nothing came out.

Ryan's gentle fingers stroked her face. "Like I told you, Lacey, you're perfect for us. And now you're ours. Forever."

And now she agreed with them. "Uh huh."

Ryan pulled up the blankets and settled in against her front, kissing her lips and hugging her tightly while Dylan nestled in against her back.

She let sleep descend as perfect happiness overtook her for the first time in her life. She'd found everything she'd ever wanted with these two men and for the first time, she was looking forward to what the future would hold.

CHAPTER EIGHTEEN

As they pulled up, Ryan saw the long hair and smiling face of his mother standing on the porch, waiting for them. He'd rung her last night to let her know what happened, and that they had Lacey at their place. She didn't know about them completing their mating, though. When she'd called this morning to invite them all up to the big house for an early dinner, he'd kept it from her. She'd enjoy the surprise after being so worried about Lacey since last night, and Lacey would enjoy his mother's excitement.

He glanced over at Lacey. "You ready, sweetheart?"

She frowned a little. "Ready for what?"

"Beautiful, look up at the house. See our mother standing there?"

She frowned as she looked out the window, "She looks worried. Why is she wringing her hands like that? Should we go?"

Ryan chuckled as Dylan barked out a laugh. "Baby, she knows about you getting hurt last night. She's no doubt driven Dad insane all night, pacing around worried about you. We're lucky she didn't come over last night."

Ryan gently cradled one of her bandaged wrists. "This is what family is all about. They care about you when you're hurt, when you're happy. They want to know. It also means they're in your face a lot."

Lacey's eyes filled with tears. "You've truly given me everything I've ever wanted."

Dylan scoffed. "You always wanted two lovers?"

Lacey's eyes went even wider and a hint of color spread over her cheeks. "Well, no, I'd never considered that. So, I guess the more accurate statement is you both have given me more than I've ever dreamed of."

Dylan's smartass comment did the trick because Lacey was smiling again. Ryan opened his door and intertwined his fingers with hers as he slid off the bench seat and dragged her to him.

"C'mon, sweetheart. Mum's going to pop an aneurism if we don't get you to her soon."

Ryan grinned broadly as he strolled up to the house, his heart about to burst with happiness. Lacey was cutely trying to stay behind him, but Dylan grabbed her other hand and tugged until she was walking between them. Anticipation of their mother's reaction to them having completed the mating had him nearly jumping out of his skin.

As they stepped up the first step, he kept his gaze locked on his mum, waiting for the moment she saw the marks on Lacey's neck. With a raised eyebrow, she looked at Ryan then over to Dylan. Ryan started laughing. He couldn't help it. Even with all the shit that went down last night, he'd mated with his beautiful Lacey and life was good. Better than good.

By the time they'd reached the porch, their mother was frowning at all of them.

"What are you two boys so damn happy about? I've been worried sick since you told me what happened to our Lacey last night. Come here, dear. I need to give you hug."

Ryan joined Dylan in releasing her hands so they could gently guide their mate into their mother's arms. Surely, this close she'd see Lacey's marks without having to be told.

Lacey held her shoulders high and her steps were stiff, but Ryan wasn't worried. He knew the moment his mother embraced Lacey, she'd relax. Their poor mate hadn't been raised in a loving home filled with hugs and affection. Ryan didn't mind making up for that now they had her. He and Dylan would constantly shower her with love in all its forms. He also knew his family would quickly embrace Lacey as one of them.

"Oh, my dear girl. You're safe now."

Ryan winced as he realized Lacey was sobbing into his mother's embrace. Damn, maybe having this family dinner today was a mistake. Too soon after the attack for her. He'd been so focused on wanting to show Lacey she had a whole family now, and of course, he wanted to show all his family that he and Dylan had claimed her.

He hadn't been making shit up when he'd told Lacey it was rare for the youngest cubs in a family to find their mate first. Generally, it happened in order from the oldest to the youngest. He mentally shook his head. Yeah, they really were blowing that tradition out of the water. Max had found his mate, too, now, thanks to Lacey, and was the fourth born. Ryan idly wondered who Max would be sharing his mate with. Since he and Dylan were twins, everyone had been certain they'd end up sharing a mate. But the other brothers could be mixed up any which way ... or they could be paired with a lion.

His chest ached in sympathy for his parents. They should have been a triad, but their third was a lion shifter who had rejected sharing his mother with a cheetah. Some days he could see the pain in his mother's gaze, as though despite how happy her life had been, she knew something was missing.

Ryan focused on Dylan. Nope, he was perfectly fine with sharing his mate with his twin. In fact, he couldn't imagine it any other way.

"C'mon, Mum. Let our mate go so we can get inside where the food is. It smells delicious."

A blush crept over his mother's cheeks as she released Lacey and started waving her hands at the boys.

"Oh, you charmers. Go on, get inside. Your brothers and father are all waiting for you."

Lacey turned her face up to Ryan, and as he leaned down to kiss her, he heard his mother's gasp. Finally!

Lacey froze mid kiss, and Ryan chuckled before he pressed a final, chaste kiss to her soft lips.

"I believe Mum has just noticed your beautiful new marks, sweetheart."

He took her hand in his as Dylan gathered her hair in his hand and lowered to kiss over his mark. She shuddered and closed her eyes for a moment.

"I'd forgotten about the bites. How will I explain them to non shifters? Two massive bite marks on either side of my throat are going to be rather hard to miss."

Dylan laughed, but he couldn't see the look in their mate's eyes. She was honestly frightened. With a gentle smile, Ryan ran his free hand over his mark on her. "Only shifters can see them, baby. They weren't real bites, but magic ones. There's no scarring in the way you're thinking. To a full human, your neck looks as beautifully flawless as it did yesterday."

"Ah, okay. All this shifter stuff is going to take some getting used to."

Now Ryan did chuckle. What would Lacey do when they had a child who could shift and climb on the roof of the house at the age of three? Now that would be an adjustment for her.

Speaking of babies, they needed to talk to her about that. As much as he'd love to start a family now, they were young and had plenty of time. With Lacey just starting a new job, he couldn't imagine her wanting to have a baby any time soon. He glanced over at her flat stomach. She would look good rounded with their cubs. A lump formed in his throat. Would they have twins? Would she want the traditional nine kids?

Dylan shoulder-bumped him.

"Quit eyeing off her belly. We're not knocking her up yet, so don't even suggest it. I want her all to us for a while first. I've heard that kids will ruin your sex life. I'm not having that happen for at least five years. Maybe longer."

"Gah, you are such a bloody caveman."

With a completely unrepentant grin, Dylan led the way into the dining room, grabbing Lacey's hand on his way to drag her in behind him. Ryan shook his head as Dylan didn't stop until he'd towed the poor woman over to where three seats had been left empty for them. Predictably, when he stopped, he pulled out her chair and let her sit down. But naturally, he didn't stop there. He knew his twin, knew the man would want everyone to know they'd mated her.

Sure enough, Dylan gathered her hair and gently pushing her head to the side, pressing a kiss to the center of his mark.

Max rose and moved to come over to them. "Holy shit! You claimed her! Congratulations!"

Before Max made it, his father beat him to Lacey and pulled her back out of the chair to give her a big bear hug. Ryan stood back, pride filling him as each one of his brothers came to give their new sister a hug, letting her know how accepted she was, and that he and Dylan hadn't lied to her about how welcoming their family would be.

When they all finally got settled back at the table, Max was sitting opposite Ryan.

"So, Dad gave you an early release, Max?"

Ryan had known that their father would never have kept Max on lockdown once he learned Max had seen his mate.

"Yep. We spoke first thing this morning, and here I am. Free as a bird."

Dylan spoke up. "And I guess you'll be shadowing us when we take Lacey back to her place to pack?"

Max grinned broadly. "Sure will. I need to find Laura, and I'm guessing the fastest way to make that happen is with you three."

"Wait. Why do you need to find Laura? Has this got something to do with the way both of you freaked out the other day when you saw each other? No, wait. Don't answer that. First, why am I packing up?"

Ryan tried not to grin but failed. He fake-coughed so he could cover his mouth with his fist. Ryan had warned his twin not to force the moving issue. Of course, like Dylan, Ryan wanted their mate in their house with them, but he was fine with living between their two houses until they settled on a routine that worked for all of them. So long as they were together, Ryan didn't mind where they were. He loved his mate, and if she needed to live with Laura a little longer in order to be happy, then they would just move in with her there.

Dylan clenched his jaw as he mentally debated how he could answer Lacey without sounding like a caveman. When after a full minute he still couldn't come up with anything, he decided to just barrel on through. "Beautiful, I assumed that now we're mated, you'd want to live with us."

Dylan released the breath he didn't realize he'd been holding when a smile curved her lips. Maybe he hadn't fucked it all up on their first day of being mated. She cupped his jaw in her palm.

"Of course, I want to live with you both. But we need to discuss where, you can't just dictate to me and expect me to fall into line. That'll never work long-term."

Well, Dylan thought it would work just fine if she simply did what he said all the time. But his mother hadn't raised him to be a fool, and he wanted Lacey to have her own mind and be brave enough to speak it to him always.

"I'm not sure I can handle living in the city, beautiful. I'm not built for it. Ryan and I need the space out here."

Lacey silenced anything else with a quick kiss. "How about to start with we live between the two? We'll stay at my place when I'm working in the office, then the rest of the time we'll stay out here? I don't want to leave

Laura with no roommate without any warning. Everything with us happened so quickly, I'm sure she wasn't expecting me to move out yet."

Max cut into their conversation, "Don't worry about Laura, Lacey. I'll make sure she's taken care of."

Lacey's eyes sparked with something that looked a lot like anger, and Dylan was glad it wasn't directed at him. She turned to glare at Max.

"Laura is my best friend, the only one who's cared about me for years. So, you'd better start explaining what the hell is going on. Especially if you want my help."

Max just gave Lacey a lazy smile, obviously not intimidated in the least at Lacey's fiery side coming out.

"She's my mate, Lacey. When I saw her at the zoo the other day, my cheetah knew instantly that she was mine. You just said that she acted out of character that day, too. That means she somehow picked up on our connection as well."

Lacey's hands snuck out, one toward Ryan and the other seeking his hand. He gladly took her palm in his and lifted it to press a kiss over the healing wound on her inner wrist. He would see that she was always protected in the future. No way would any other asshole get close enough to hurt his mate ever again.

"Um. Do all cheetah shifters end up in ménages?"

"Pretty much. Unless something happens to one of the men and it leaves a couple behind."

Dylan winced at his father's strained words. There should have been two fathers in their family, but the stupid lion had refused to share with a cheetah. Instead, the fool decided to go old-school and challenge his father for their mate. Obviously, their dad won, but it was a damn shitty way to start a mating, that's for sure.

"Who else will be Laura's mate? One of you, or someone else?"

"Hopefully another of my sons will be her mate. Most likely Jed or Kane, as they are closest in age to Max. But you never know. Perhaps a party for your engagement, assuming you are also going to follow human traditions along with shifter ones, will allow all the boys to test for a connection with your friend?"

Lacey nodded then started chuckling. Dylan frowned. What was funny about that?

"Why is having a party funny? I don't get it."

"Oh, it's not the party that's funny. It's the fact that when you first told me you wanted to share me, I spoke to her about it in vague terms. Asking what she would do if she met someone who wanted an unconventional relationship. And she said love is love and it didn't matter what form it came in, if you find it, you latch onto it. She also said that she wasn't sure how far she'd go to keep a man if she found one that was halfway decent. So, I was laughing because I was just thinking about how she'll react to the whole shifters-are-real thing along with the fact she'll have two mates for life. Her reaction is going to be priceless."

Dylan beamed with happiness. He loved his mate's slightly offbeat sense of humor. He didn't think normal chicks would find it amusing that their friend was about to fall down a rabbit hole of new realities, but his Lacey did. His mother came into the room armed with a couple of bottles of champagne before Max could respond.

"Max, be a dear and fetch the flutes for me. We need to celebrate me finally getting a daughter. Trust me, Lacey. After raising nine boys, I need some more estrogen around this place."

As the drinks were poured, Dylan sat back and focused on his mate. She was stunningly beautiful and looked beyond happy as she sat there chatting with his mother. The whole time she talked, she made sure to keep a hand on both him and Ryan, like she needed the connection. He couldn't believe how much her touch settled him. They'd only met what, a week ago? Two? And here they were happily mated and set to spend the rest of their lives together.

When all the glasses had been poured and handed out, Dylan reluctantly released Lacey's hand so she could drink hers. He slid his palm over her thigh to keep a connection with her before he raised his glass to toast their gorgeous mate with the high end champagne their mother kept hidden away for just such occasions.

Dylan addressed the room, his heart bursting with pride, "To our Lacey, the most perfect mate any pair of shifters could ask for."

Her eyes filled with tears as she smiled broadly and blushed at his toast. Yep, he and Ryan were one lucky pair of males, that was for sure.

EPILOGUE

Six months later

The newspaper's photographer flashed a photo of her as she stepped up to the aisle with Laura beside her. It would be her friend's turn to officially tie the knot next month. She gave the photographer a smile as he snapped another shot.

It was so lovely of the newspaper to offer to put her wedding in the celebrations pages, Especially since she was still considered one of the newbies at the paper.

Everything was settled now. Cameron's rescue and her subsequent story afterwards had caught the interest of the papers' readers, but everyone seemed happy to accept her hinting that the cat part of the story was nothing more than the imagination of a young boy finding a way to help him cope with the traumatic situation he'd found himself in.

The outcome had worked out for everyone, and the shifters remained unknown to the general population. Her boss had loved her story and that had helped cement her place at the paper. And to top it all off, she also now part of the most amazing family she could ever dream of.

Dylan and Ryan had been her mates for six months, but today they would celebrate their loving bond in a more traditional, human way, in the small church their family had attended for generations.

The church was buzzing with voices, new friends and many old. The Monaghan family was bigger than she'd imagined, all of them fully accepting the triad the three of them created. Probably because most of them were also a part of a triad.

The twins' parents were actually the odd ones out in this crowd.

She took a deep breath and nodded at Laura. "Ready?"

Her best friend laughed softly at her. "Aren't I supposed to ask you that?"

Lacey shrugged. For her, this was more for his parents than anyone else. As far as she was concerned, she'd married them six months ago on their mating night.

"I'm so ready for this. Let's do it."

The music sounded, and a smile lifted her lips. The traditional wedding march to mark the occasion.

Laura turned around, and like the perfect maid of honor she was, gripped her flowers and began walking down the aisle with complete poise and grace. You'd never guess the woman was way more comfortable in combat boots and jeans.

Lacey took a moment to breathe and looked down at her own small bouquet of lilacs. Everything was perfect, an accurate reflection of how her life was now.

So much had changed in so little time. She was safe and happy, for the first time in her memory. Rodney had been given a two-year jail term for stalking and abducting her but would probably get out earlier on good behavior. However, when he got released, he wasn't allowed anywhere near her, or he'd get tossed back in. Assuming he'd survive her men if he was stupid enough to come near her.

She shook those dark thoughts out of her head and stepped out from behind the pillar, facing her men and the minister that stood at the front of the church waiting for her arrival.

She smiled at them as she began her own slow walk, towards her men, and into her future.

With each step, she reflected on her love for them and theirs for her. Thanks to Dylan and Ryan, she wasn't worried about anything bad happening. If and when the time came to deal with Rodney again, she'd be fine. Because as long as the two men she loved with her whole heart and soul were by her side she'd always be safe.

She took the final step and handed her flowers to Laura, so she had both hands free. She wished she was marrying both her mates, but the law forbade it. And she could just imagine the field day her newspaper would have with that story.

She took Dylan's hand. As the older, by a few minutes, his parents had suggested he be her legal husband, while her beautiful Ryan was the best man, a step behind his twin. She looked over Dylan's shoulder and met Ryan's eyes, giving him her biggest smile. They all knew they had an equal partnership, and Ryan had assured her that as long as she was committed to him and took their last name, he didn't mind whose name was on the paperwork.

"Ready?" Dylan asked her, squeezing both of her hands, and giving her his characteristically cheeky smile.

"Always."

They turned as one and stepped forward, facing the minister in front of them.

"Dearly beloved..."

As Lacey heard the age-old words and they spoke their vows and exchanged rings, Lacey's hands trembled, and the tears flowed unexpectedly. Even though she'd completed her mating months ago, this moment in time was her traditional symbol that she was married. The little girl inside of her was truly content to be standing in a church, wearing a fancy white dress and holding her husband's hand.

After her lonely childhood, she'd never even known this kind of love existed, let alone that she'd be lucky enough to experience it. But here she was, with the love of her two men. Mirror image twins that completed her mind, body and soul.

The End

About Author

Khloe Wren

Passionate, Riveting Romance That Steals Your Heart

USA Today bestselling author, Khloe Wren, lives in rural South Australia with her husband, two daughters and an ever-changing list of animals! She started writing in 2013 and has published over 30 books in the romantic suspense genre since then. She writes both paranormal and contemporary stories, including her best-selling series The Charon MC. Khloe enjoys writing outside of the box and loves her heroes strong, and her heroines even stronger.

Khloe loves hearing from readers so please reach out and connect with her:
For a free copy of Claiming Tiny, sign up for her newsletter:
https://newsletter.khloewren.com/sign_up
For a full list of all her books, check her website:
http://www.khloewren.com
For bonus content and other goodies, check out her street team:
https://www.facebook.com/groups/856383344460514/
Other social media:
FaceBook page: http://www.facebook.com/authorkhloewren
FaceBook profile: https://www.facebook.com/khloe.wren.3/
Instagram: https://www.instagram.com/khloewren/

Other books by Khloe Wren:
Paranormal Romantic Suspense:
RBMC: South Australia: #1 Spark's Rising; #2 Croc's Pledge
Iron Hammers MC: #1 Cujo's Rampage
Fire and Snow Series: #1 Guardian's Heart; #2 Noble Guardian; # 3 Guardian's Shadow; #4 Fierce Guardian; #5 Necessary Alpha; #6 Protective Instincts

Single Titles: FireStarter; The Warrior, The Witch & The Wombat; Scarred Perfection; Destiny Realized (Bad Alpha Anthology); Mirror Image Seduction; Deception
Contemporary Romantic Suspense:
Charon MC: #1 Inking Eagle; #2 Fighting Mac; #3 Chasing Taz; #4 Claiming Tiny; #5 Saving Scout; #6 Tripping Nitro; #7 Scout's Legacy; #8 Mac's Destiny; #9 Losing Bash; #10 Finding Needles; #11 Forging Blade; #12 Taming Keys; #13 Breaking Arrow
Kings of Sydney: #1 Daniil
Single Titles: Fireworks; Scandals: Zeck

About Author

Tamsin Baker

Happily Ever Afters. Dirty Words. Sweet Love.

Tamsin Baker loves everything passionate and beautiful. Her books can be long, short and everything in between. But they're all fast paced with snappy dialogue and lots of sex.
She wants her books to be everything that a fictional world can be — full of happily ever afters, dirty words and sweet love. 'Love is love' and she tries to show that in a range of sub genres. From m/m contemporary to paranormal ménage.
In real life she has a need to shock people and bring up embarrassing topics at the most inappropriate times.

Tamsin loves hearing from readers so please reach out and connect with her:
For a free copy of 'Loving the High Warlock, sign up for her newsletter: https://dl.bookfunnel.com/pbzg4vuf4e
For a full list of all her books, check her website: https://www.erotictamsinbaker.com/
Other social media:
FaceBook page: https://www.facebook.com/Tamsin-Baker-317614138351036
FaceBook profile: https://www.facebook.com/tamsin.baker.754/

Other books by Tamsin Baker:
Paranormal Steamy Romance:
Perfect Pairs series: #1 Prowling their Mate; #2 Stalking their Mate; #3 Shadowing their Mate
Dragon Masters Series: #1 Princess Tattiena; #2 Warrior Nakeeri
The Borough Boys Series: #1 Grayson's Mate; #2 Aaron's Mate; # 3 Brad's Mate; #4 Megan's Mate

New World Shifters: #1 The Omega Shift; #2 Saving the Omega; # 3 The Alpha's Omega Mate
The Blood World Series: #1 Wolf Mated; #2 Dragon Mated; # 3 Vampire Mated; #4 Shadow's Quest
Shifters of the Land, Sea and Air: #1 Finding Destiny; #2 Knowing Destiny; # 3 Swimming Destiny
The Final Piece: #1 Eternal Hearts; #2 Bonded Hearts; # 3 Healed Hearts
Contemporary Romance:
Melbourne Men: #1 Danny's Coming Out; #2 Tommy's Bear
Single Titles: Truth be Told; Too Busy for Love; Impossible Desire; His Fireman, #Gay; His City Boy; Her Vampire Mates; The Alpha in Her

www.ingramcontent.com/pod-product-compliance
Lightning Source LLC
Chambersburg PA
CBHW070326120726
47909CB00008B/2611